He was standing maybe twenty feet away, just behind a pair of feet angular gravestones. Despite the heat, he was dressed in a heavy woolen overcoat with a wine-colored scarf wrapped around his throat and a green plaid pork pie hat pulled down low over his brow. His face didn't look so much like a face as a distended, pallid balloon that was slowly deflating, going flaccid and loose, set with bulbous pouches. It was the color and texture of pork chop fat...white, greasy, blubbery. Christina gasped, felt a white heat spread through her limbs, a rubbery weakness in her joints.

It was a dead, gas-bloated face cut by a grinning mouth like a knife slash in white rubber. The eyes were soft gray oysters sinking in brine. He was staring at her, smiling, flies lighting off him.

He cradled something in the crook of one arm, too, she saw. Was it a baby? It was wrapped in a loose brown blanket that looked quite dirty. It was moving with worming gyrations. She had the terrible feeling that if he uncovered it, it would be much like him...a plump white maggot.

CORPSE RIDER

TIM CURRAN

1

It started the day she visited her mother's grave.

It was one of those high midsummer afternoons, pale yellow and perfectly dry, the sun balanced overhead like a dripping wax coin. The only sound was the dry crunching of the grass and the drone of grasshoppers. No breeze, no suggestion of one, just that heavy air, like something blown from a foundry pit.

Christina walked amongst the tombstones and carefully trimmed hedges, the wilting lilies in her hand dying with a sickly-sweet odor of decay. The cemetery was wide and flat like saltpan desert, cut by a few paved roads and an occasional stand of sagging maple or elm. A spreading orchard of marble held in check by a meandering wrought-iron fence.

In the distance, she could see other forms tending graves and mourning loved ones, but they were lost in the shimmering haze. She was alone, feeling the sighing emptiness around her, ever aware of the magnetism of her mother's grave. She found it without really making a concerted effort, even though she had not been there in three years. There was a guilt associated with that, a heaviness, a despair that filled her with lost voices. The stone was russet in color, set flat in straw-dry shorn grasses.

MOTHER, it said.

She repeated the word in her mind, painfully aware that time had robbed it of its import and magnitude. She kneeled at the edge of the grave, her eyes wide and misty, white teeth showing through the pink slit of her mouth.

Well, I'm here, Doris, she found herself thinking, *now what?*

She waited for great emotions and deep, wrenching sentiments to fill her, but there were none. A sense of loss, of time blowing away childhood memories like fallen leaves, but not much else. That made her feel even more guilty, of course, because there should have been something deep and meaningful but there simply wasn't.

She chewed her lower lip, unable to adequately catalog what she was feeling. They hadn't been close after she left home and even before that things were strained and distant. Doris—funny, but her mother had always been *Doris*, never Mom—was from a different world, an alien place where the only aspirations a woman had were a husband and children. She wanted Christina to be like that, a mere extension of her man, a baby-machine that kept house and cooked and lived vicariously through her significant other. And in keeping with that, she had tried to marry her off at least half a dozen times before her death.

And maybe had Christina been weaker, it would have happened.

Christina sat there, picturing Doris, knowing that she would have been disappointed that at thirty, her daughter still was not married and had no hopes of starting a family. But it wasn't as if she hadn't tried. She'd fallen in love three times in the last four years and each time her betrothed had been unfaithful. It seemed that the law of averages would have been against something like that. Three heartbreaks later, she felt desolate and barren inside, a fallow field left untended and abandoned.

I tried, Christina thought. *But sorry, mother of mine, three strikes and you're out. I can't go through it again. At least not for a while.*

And that was the truth.

She simply wasn't up to the dating scene because all the trust had been squeezed out of her and what was left behind was cold and lonely and possibly empty, but it was also *safe*. There was no chance of pain, no flirtation with disaster. There was just the uneasy silence of solitude. And unless her mother could still pull some matrimonial strings from beyond the pale, it just wasn't going to happen.

Christina stood up.

She couldn't bear this.

Doris had made her feel guilty in life and now it seemed even worse after death. Sighing, she turned away and noticed a single gravestone set on a weedy plot. Now, why would they allow that to happen? Even if the deceased had no surviving relatives, shouldn't the groundskeeper take care of things like this? She went over there, feeling...well, she wasn't exactly sure what she was feeling. Something like pity? Remorse for someone she had never even known? Maybe, but mostly a sort of melancholy that this person—long dead—had been forgotten.

The stone was old and gray, flecked with lichen.

CHARLES DAVID SLICK
1907—1956
BELOVED SON

It was leaning badly to one side and a mutiny of weeds had grown up around its base. Although Christina did not say the word *disgraceful* out loud—it was too much like something Doris would have said—she thought it. Kneeling down, she plucked the weeds out in handfuls. When she was done and she had a pile of dead grasses and assorted scrub weeds at her knees, she wondered why she had bothered at all. It wasn't any of her business and she didn't even know the family or anyone named Slick for that matter.

She set the lilies up against the stone. "There," she said. "Just so you know you're not forgotten."

It made her feel good about herself for a moment or two...then a chill crawled up the nape of her neck as if someone had exhaled a cold breath down her back.

I'm being watched.

She sat up quickly, looking around, searching for that intrusive, evasive set of spying eyes. But there was no one, just the regiments of headstones winding off into the distance, a few bees lighting off funeral sprays. The breath in her lungs felt scorched, sweat ran down her spine. She felt hot and cold as if she might pitch right over if she tried to stand.

She saw no one, but that gnawing sense of visitation scraped along the back of her neck.

You're being ridiculous, can't you see that? There's no one here

But there was.

Somehow, some way, there was another.

A man...or something like one.

He was standing maybe twenty feet away, just behind a pair of rectangular gravestones. Despite the heat, he was dressed in a heavy woolen overcoat with a wine-colored scarf wrapped around his throat and a green plaid pork pie hat pulled down low over his brow. His face didn't look so much like a face as a distended, pallid balloon that was slowly deflating, going flaccid and loose, set with bulbous pouches. It was the color and texture of pork chop fat...white, greasy, blubbery. Christina gasped, felt a white heat spread through her limbs, a rubbery weakness in her joints.

It was a dead, gas-bloated face cut by a grinning mouth like a knife slash in white rubber. The eyes were soft gray oysters sinking in brine.

He was staring at her, smiling, flies lighting off him.

He cradled something in the crook of one arm, too, she saw. Was it a baby? It was wrapped in a loose brown blanket that looked quite dirty. It was moving with worming gyrations. She had the terrible feeling that if he uncovered it, it would be much like him…a plump white maggot.

She was breathing so hard by that point, she began to hyperventilate.

The man kept smiling and staring, secreting a rank and gassy stench like rotting cabbage. He brought up his free hand and waved, his fingers swollen-up like sausages. It was the waterlogged hand of a corpse pulled from a river.

The thing under the blanket was writhing as if it wanted to be free. She had the most awful feeling that he wanted her to look at it. That he wanted her to *hold* it.

"So kind," he said with a mushy sound, as if his mouth was filled with something soft, like pudding. "So caring. What a fine mother you shall be."

Christina thought she would scream but she didn't. The world spun around her and she pitched over into the grass, oblivious to everything but the spiraling nightmares in her head.

2

When she came to, a set of hands gripped her and she began to scream. She thought for certain that the dead man had taken hold of her, perhaps to drag her off to some silk-lined marriage bed. Completely irrational, she fought and clawed and shrieked.

"Easy!" a voice said. "Just take it easy!"

It was then that she realized where she was and what she was doing. She stopped fighting. The guy who was holding her was definitely not the dead man. In fact, he was a very ordinary man in all respects. He was dressed in green workpants with soil stains at the knee, a matching cap on his head. He was holding her with huge, callused hands, his sunburned face deeply-etched with lines.

"I'm not here to hurt you. I was down a ways and saw you fold-up, so I came over to help. Just tell me what I can do."

His voice and his bearing were sincere. She figured he was a hearty seventy if he was a day and there was something almost fatherly about him. He released her and she pulled away a few feet, wanting to say something that would make sense of the situation but knowing all that would come out were feeble lies.

"I'm Frank Betts," he said. "I'm the caretaker here. Do you need medical help?"

"No, no...I'm fine."

It was obvious that he didn't believe that any more than she did.

"My shack's just over there. Why don't you come with me and I'll get you something cool to drink."

Christina shook her head and not because she didn't think it was a kind offer but because she doubted her legs would carry her that far. She needed a few minutes. Frank just waited there. He produced a cigarette, said, "Mind?" She shook her head and he lit up, exhaling smoke and staring off across the expanse of tombstones. He was watching her without really watching her and she knew it. Her dad used to do that. There was something touching about it.

He dragged off his cigarette. "Damn heat. It'll get the best of you. Starts feeling heavy on your shoulders after a time. It'll drive anyone to their knees sooner or later."

But not you, I bet, Christina thought, taking in his broad shoulders and massive chest. Like a tree, he was built to withstand the worst weather.

As he smoked, looking a bit uncomfortable, she looked around the cemetery. *Did I really see that...that man?* She wasn't so sure now. She wanted to believe it was just the heat but she knew better. Something had happened. Something fantastic. She wasn't the sort to go around fainting like a heroine in a Victorian novel.

Before she could stop herself, she said, "I saw someone."

Frank didn't look at her. "Did you?"

"Yes," she said. "I saw a man standing over there and he looked... well, he didn't look right. In fact, he looked like he was dead."

She expected him to start laughing or at least to roll his eyes, dismissing her as an over-imaginative female. He did neither. He blew smoke out. His eyes were the color of steel wool. "Probably the heat. It can make you see things that aren't there. It's happened to me lots of times. You work here long enough, sometimes you see things out of the corner of your eye...figures standing about...but when you look, there's nothing there."

Christina wanted to be incensed at his dismissal, but she wasn't. And mainly because it wasn't really a dismissal at all. *He sees things, too.* It wasn't an outright confession, but it alluded to one.

She felt like she might be able to stand again. She breathed in and out, grabbing her mother's stone and steadying herself. Frank helped her up the rest of the way.

"I'm not a hysterical female," she said.

"Never said you were."

She smiled thinly. "Well, that's one up on me. If someone told me they'd seen a ghost, that's exactly what I would have thought."

"What makes you think it was a ghost?" he asked in all sincerity.

"I wouldn't know what else to call it. I saw it and I smelled it. It was nasty."

Frank nodded, staring over at the Slick grave. He pursed his lips and she could clearly hear him grinding his teeth as if from anxiety. "Somebody pulled all the weeds," he said. "Would that someone be you?"

She shrugged. "Yes...I...I don't know. It looked uncared for so I just pulled them. I'm not sure why."

He nodded again, crushing out his cigarette between his thumb and forefinger. He didn't even seem to feel it. "I get busy and sometimes the older graves, those with no family left to call, get forgotten about for a time. It's no excuse, but it happens." He tucked the cigarette butt into a Ziploc bag he carried in his pocket. "Now and again, someone like you comes along and tidies things."

"Is that...is that a problem?"

"No, no I don't suppose so." He was making a point of not meeting her eyes now. "Just surprised me is all. Nobody ever comes to tend the Slick grave. Nobody has in a long time. Nobody but you."

She was going to tell him that she hadn't come for that specific purpose, but with a wave of his hand he was off, threading amongst the headstones. She stood there awhile longer until she felt a chill, then she left in a hurry.

3

The human mind is a funny thing.

A machine in constant blurring motion, spinning tales and weaving absurdities, creating and destroying, making you believe the most awful things and then canceling them out hours later with a pen slash of logic and reason. And that's how it was for Christina the evening after she'd visited her mother's grave—fairy dust was sprinkled in her head, then blown away before it took hold. She left the cemetery in a state of shock, webbed in fright, as close to the teetering rim of madness as she'd ever been or dared to be. She fought blindly through traffic until she was home and the door was locked. As she sat there, trembling and pouring straight Absolut down her throat, she told herself she had just been haunted, that she had seen a living corpse.

But as the minutes passed and the vodka performed its magic, leveling her out and sweeping the accumulated dung from her mind, she began to think differently. The wheels of her brain screeched to a halt, jumped tracks and began moving in a totally different direction. And it was the sort of direction she could live with. A safe direction, a sane direction.

That guy you saw, her mind told her, he was not a dead man...you know that, don't you? The dead do not walk and all that...blah, blah, blah, it's make-believe, you're old enough to know better. Okay. He was just some weirdo⊚

Weirdo? That was a spook. A goddamned spook. There were more worms in him than a bait shop. He was a corpse, a walking corpse.

No, he was not, Christina. Now listen to me on this (she loved this voice; it treated her not only like a stupid hysterical female, but a very *young*, impressionable, and stupid hysterical female). What you saw was no spook. It was very hot. You suffered heat stroke, you⊚

Oh, come on.

All right then, what else could it be? Do you really believe spooks flit about and in the middle of the afternoon of all things?

Either I was haunted or I've gone irretrievably mad.

Or you imagined it. Or it was some kind of twisted joke perpetrated by person or persons unknown. Or, maybe you just saw some weirdo and *thought* he looked all bloated-up and white.

She sat there, wrung out, sucking down vodka, feeling equally terrified and foolish. Maybe what it really, ultimately came down to was one of those freakish, unexplainable events that people sometimes had. If you could re-create it under laboratory conditions, put it under the microscope and dissect it with a very fucking sharp knife…well, then you might make sense of it.

Maybe. Possibly.

She liked that. Maybe it was strictly vodka logic, but it worked for her. Something in the cluttered back of her mind told her she was jumping to the thinnest possible rationalization, but it wasn't saying it *too* loudly and Christina certainly wasn't listening.

She was feeling better.

The Absolut would have it no other way. Besides, she wasn't even sure if she believed in God, let alone ghosts.

She handled this new skein of logic, ran it through her hands and liked its feel, its texture, knew it would be easy to spin into a security blanket. One that would easily keep the chill of the spookies off her.

So that's how she spent her night, drinking and talking to the TV set, making smartass comments first to an old Katherine Hepburn movie and later to Steven Seagal as he kicked ass on ten or fifteen bikers without breaking a sweat. Morning and her alarm clock found her on the couch, the TV still on, the inside of her mouth coated with something like belly button lint. The vodka was still there, too, true blue and faithful, banging a gong in her head and filling her belly with acid.

When she got to work, slipped into her little cubicle ten minutes late, sucked down some coffee and checked her email, Nancy stuck her head in and said, "You look like shit."

"Thanks for noticing."

"Just thought you'd want to know."

The day wound out like any other. It found its groove, sluggish and loopy at first, but eventually picking up speed and then it was just another day. Bob, her supervisor, kept bringing in more orders for textbooks and Christina entered them into the system. In other cubicles, her co-workers ran down people behind their backs and the canned Muzak played, and from time to time Nancy stuck her head in and made some smart comment. Nothing out of the ordinary. Christina lost herself in her work and although she would have been the first to admit that her job was tedious, dull, and repetitive, she didn't complain that day. She buried herself in her work and didn't even look for a shovel at lunch break.

By two that afternoon, she was no longer even sure any of it had happened. Maybe she had hallucinated it and maybe she needed a good long rest. Regardless, when her mail came, was dumped on her table by the new gopher, she barely paid any attention to it.

An hour later, she sorted through it and found a pink envelope.

She opened it and there was a small card inside. On the cover was a watercolor illustration of some posies sprouting from the earth. Above them was printed, DEAREST MOTHER. Christina sat there staring at it, wondering, wondering. She opened it and it said, FROM YOUR DEVOTED ONE. No signature, no nothing. The card itself was soiled and there was a dirty thumbprint on the inside like whoever had handled it had just drained the oil from a transmission or

Finished digging a grave.

Christina dropped the card on her desk, something like a long, sharp screw twisting in her belly.

4

What she didn't need were any social obligations.

But Nancy remembered their date for the new Ben Stiller comedy and despite every attempt to get out of it, Christina found herself in a movie theater that evening while Nancy ate popcorn next to her and everyone laughed at the appropriate moments. Christina didn't laugh. The movie was probably funny, but she couldn't make sense of it. In fact, she couldn't follow the plot for more than thirty seconds at a crack.

What she kept thinking was: *That card means absolutely nothing. It can't mean anything. Just because there was a dirty print on it does not mean the person who sent it came out of a grave.*

Logic. Reason. Oh, how hard they tried to again derail the train of her mania, but she wasn't taking the bait and the hook wasn't sharp enough to catch her. So she sat in the theater, feeling completely hollowed out like somebody had dug a ditch in her (or a grave) and she had been sucked down into its depths, powerless and hopeless, tucked away somewhere dark and crowded where the sunshine could never reach.

Paralyzed, completely paralyzed.

No other word could hope to sum it up quite so succinctly. She had the oddest sense that some game was being played and she was part of it, only the rules were unknown to her. They would only be shared on a need-to-know basis. And the idea of that made her feel like a blank piece of paper waiting to be written on.

Just a card, just a dirty card. That's all it was.

Yet, she knew it was so much more.

DEAREST MOTHER. FROM YOUR DEVOTED ONE.

So kind. So caring. What a fine mother you shall be.

The memory of those words and the horrible thing that had spoken them made her want to scream out loud right there in the theater. She had to grip the arms of her chair so she didn't completely lose it. She felt like she was on a roller coaster slowly ascending the first big hill, then plummeting down, down into the darkness.

Oh, Christ in heaven…what does it mean? What does any of it mean?

The movie ended and Nancy insisted they go out for a bite of pizza as they always did, only Christina had no appetite. She had little desire to do anything but sit and stare and wonder. Nancy was always good company. She and Christina had a good relationship at work that spilled into their off hours, but tonight it just wasn't working. Christina felt like a rotten tooth waiting to be pulled.

Nancy kept asking her what was wrong, kept trying to find that nerve and work it, but Christina would not let her anywhere near it. It was too private. Too…horrible. Nancy was a good soul. She made jokes, smartassed comments, tried anything to break through Christina's shell, but it just wasn't happening.

"You know," she finally said, "I've had yeast infections that were better company than you."

Christina almost laughed at that one. She actually reached up for the sunlight of companionship, but at the last moment it all came back to her, sinking her, pulling down the shade and leaving her trembling in the darkness.

She didn't know too much about Nancy. Just the basics and that was enough. They had worked together for five years and saw movies together. Nancy was small and blonde and tough, very buxom; whereas Christina herself was tall and dark and willowy. She suspected that Nancy was a lesbian or was considering the idea and she was fine with that. Nancy had been through a bad marriage. She liked to joke that when she'd said, *I do,* her ex-husband had took that to mean, *I do want to be shit on.* She never dated. She rarely socialized outside of movie nights with Christina. Her failed marriage was like a canker sore on her gums, one her tongue kept investigating again and again, unable to keep away despite the pain it brought.

When she talked about her private life at all, it was usually the marriage. She had a past, of course, but she didn't like to discuss it, other than with a few offhand self-deprecating remarks or to say that the last time she'd had good sex, she'd gone through ten bucks worth of batteries and had trouble sitting down for three days.

But that was Nancy.

That was her charm.

Finally, they gave it up, abandoning the thin crust pepperoni, much to Nancy's heartbreak, and went back to Christina's apartment. She did not want company, but at the same time, she was desperately frightened to be alone.

When they pulled up across from Christina's building, Nancy said, "You're not trying to get me up there to take advantage of me, are you?"

"Yes," Christina said. "The truth is out."

"Well, you've been a shitty date all around. You better be really good in the sack or I want my money back."

"Well, if three failed relationships are any clue◎"

"C'mon, Christy, I was kidding. Don't brood."

"I feel very...broody."

"Is that actually a word?"

"It is tonight."

Nancy tried to keep the banter going, but Christina just wasn't in the mood. She had indeed invited Nancy up for a reason and that was because she had a very nasty feeling that something was about to happen. Something she was not up to facing alone and something it might be good for another to witness. A psychological litmus test. An am-I-crazy-or-not sort of thing.

I've got to make her stay. Whatever it takes, I can't be alone tonight.

As they climbed the stairs, the feeling of dread grew.

It set down roots, swelling and thriving, filling Christina's belly with scraping branches and macabre blooms that made her want to fall down and cry. It was bad. It was really bad. If it all didn't come crashing to a halt one way or another, she was going to have a nervous breakdown.

"Well, well, well," Nancy said grabbing something that was dangling from the doorknob. "What's this? Did you leave it on someone's nightstand or is it a gift?"

She was holding a gold necklace with a cameo pendant hooked to it. No, it was not Christina's and it certainly was no gift. Maybe a curse or a hex, but certainly not a gift. It was dirty and tarnished like it had been hidden away in the darkness for too long, maybe in a box.

Nancy dropped it into Christina's hand and it felt cold, looping in her palm like a worm. Her hand shook so badly she could barely hold it. She opened it. Dirt fell out. Inside, in an elegant antique scroll it read, MOTHER, DEARLY BELOVED.

Christina saw it and a shrill moan came unbidden from her throat. She felt her head spin, felt those wild and grim growths in her belly climb up the back of her throat, cutting off her air. "I wonder," she heard herself say, "whose casket this came from...whose neck it was wrapped around..."

And then she pitched straight over, going out cold.

5

She couldn't really remember much of it later.

There was a blackness in her mind, smooth and murky like the surface of an ancient mirror blackened by lithograph crayon. No amount of rubbing could clean it or show her the reflection of that dire memory.

When she opened her eyes, she was on the couch and Nancy was there, dabbing her forehead with a cool, moist cloth. "You know, if I have to bodily carry you around, I think the least you can do is tell me why I'm doing it."

Christina opened her mouth, but couldn't seem to find her voice. It had fallen down deep inside her, into the murk of a bottomless black well.

Nancy made her drink from a water bottle. "Okay," she said. "Whenever you're ready."

Christina found her voice, but feared what it would say. She was terrified to set it loose and let it sketch out the madness of the past twenty-four hours, so she merely said, "I've been through some…shit."

"Mmm-hmm, I gathered that. Does this particular shit have a name?"

"It's not a man or anything like that."

Nancy told her she thought maybe she was shagging a gravedigger with what she'd said before passing out. But Christina could remember nothing of it. Like the final, fateful moments before a car accident, it had been wiped clean, nothing but a swath of dimness to mark its passing. She remembered coming up the stairs. Remembered the anticipation, the dread of knowing things and not knowing them at all. Then the necklace. The sense that a forest was filling her belly. Then…nothing. A blankness that was smooth and non-reflective.

"Okay," Nancy said. "Okay. It's not a man. Sometimes bad things don't have penises…it happens, just rarely. What is it then?"

Christina flinched at the idea of voicing any of it. It was as if Nancy wanted her to slit open her belly, yank her guts out so they could be examined. That's exactly what it felt like.

"C'mon, Christy."

"I saw something."

"Did you?"

Christina nodded, studying her hands. They lay in her lap like dying funeral lilies. "Yes. It was yesterday…I went to Mother's grave."

Nancy sighed. *"Mother's?* Is that what you said? Jesus Christ, Christy, I love you like an old pair of shoes, I love you as much as I can love something that doesn't take batteries…but *Mother?* Christ, you sound like Norman Bates' fucked up twin sister."

"I don't know why I said that."

And she didn't, not really. Her mother had always been Doris. Even when she was a child she called her Doris. Never…*Mother.*

"I'm sorry, Christy. It just…well, it sounds terribly Victorian or something." Nancy patted her hand. "Just ignore my mouth. My ex said it was only good for one thing…maybe he was right. Go figure. Now tell me what happened."

Christina told her. And in telling, she found that there really wasn't much there. The encounter at the cemetery had been very brief. And the bit with the card…again, brief. And now the necklace. She almost felt foolish saying these things out loud, letting someone else examine the full bloom of her paranoia. But she said it and now it was out and she couldn't call it back.

"Okay, okay, gimme a minute on this," Nancy said. "Okay, I've had my minute…are you doing drugs?"

Christina chewed her lip, looked down at her hands again. She wanted to cry and maybe she needed to, but she was simply dry inside.

"Dear God, you're serious, aren't you?" Nancy shook her head. "This is weird shit, honey. You saw a ghost or something like one…my God. I'm sorry if I'm being less than sensitive here, but this is wild shit. Say it again, tell me what you saw."

Christina stared off into space. "I saw a ghost."

"That's what I thought you said."

"If you think this is funny, Nancy, do me a little white favor and use that door over there, all right? Because I've been going through hell and I'm not really up to your urbane fucking wit."

Nancy opened her mouth, then closed it. "Okay. I had that coming. I apologize. Now let's think this through rationally. Let's figure it out together."

And that's what they did.

They approached it from all the usual directions, taking the same well-worn paths that Christina herself had been tramping down since it happened. And those paths always led to the same place—could it have been a hallucination? Some kind of temporary delirium? Something atmospheric, a trick of the light maybe? And did the card and the necklace actually have anything to do with the...*apparition* she had seen?

"Yes, they're connected," Christina said. "The mother thing. Don't ask me to make sense of it."

"I wouldn't."

"So where does any of this get us?"

"Absolutely nowhere, I'm afraid. But I'm sure you're telling me the truth."

"And?"

Nancy shrugged. "I think you saw a ghost."

Christina was getting frustrated with this crap, it was like the introduction to Logic 101, chapter one in the texts: *NO SHIT, REALLY?*

"Well, I feel so much better now," she said. "We've arrived at the facts. I'm not crazy and I'm not lying. I really saw a ghost."

"C'mon, Christy, no attitude, okay? I'm just trying to lay some groundwork here so we *can* figure this out."

"What should we do?"

"Nothing. Because there's nothing we can do. No, don't look at me like that. Just listen. If something's going on, then it'll continue to happen, right? If not, then this will fade away and leave you scratching your head. You can mark it down to one of those improbable, freakish random events like seeing a UFO or Bigfoot or my ex actually sending an alimony check."

"Again, Nancy, this isn't funny."

Nancy looked very sober. "No, it's not. It's fucking spooky is what it is. But, like I said, all we can do is wait and see, okay? There's nothing else to do. We can't go to the cops. They wouldn't buy the ghost thing and they wouldn't buy the card and the necklace. There's just no threat implied by either one. And they'd be right...we need more."

"Like what? Some rattling chains? A jar of ectoplasm?"

Nancy shrugged. "Yeah, something along that order, like it or not."

6

Nancy ended up staying the night.

Nothing happened.

Christina knew nothing would happen.

Maybe Nancy possessed some sort of arcane protective magic and maybe it was something else. Christina figured Nancy was not part of it, she had not been invited to the game and she was not allowed to play. What would happen would not happen in her presence. Just a feeling, but like glue, it stuck and Christina believed it.

So, they went to work together and wrapped themselves around the day, let it take hold of them and bury them in its usual trivialities. Which it did and did quite effectively. And despite the terror hanging from the bottom of her soul like a gorging leech, there were times when Christina actually forgot about it. When the weight of the day crushed it out of her. The office was its usual self…crazy, confused, tiresome, and it was a wonder anything got done and the company stayed afloat. But it did and its worker ants were an industrious lot, taking orders and entering them into the system, making corrections, setting print runs, and hoping it all made some sense at the warehouse. Which it rarely did. Nancy kept as busy as the others, but she spent a lot of time looking in on Christina, seeing if she was okay.

By noon, Christina was beginning to feel like she was being mothered or put on suicide watch. And maybe it was both and neither and maybe Nancy was more than a little worried about her state of mind.

At lunchtime, Christina couldn't take it anymore.

She volunteered for the lunch run.

Twelve sandwiches, six salads, three cheeseburgers. She scribbled it on her pad and got the hell out of the office, leaving Nancy's watchful eyes behind. Tom Corlyle in purchasing tried to chat it up with her on her way out, always on the hunt for spreadable legs, but Christina just politely ignored him as always and then she was on the elevator with a bunch of suits from the fifth floor, shills that smelled of money and greased palms.

It wasn't until she reached the parking garage, second floor, that she began to feel it again. It came on her as it had that day at the cemetery, that invasive sense of being watched that she simply could not shake. It was on her and in her and she stood in the echoing vault of the garage, just waiting for it.

A car passed.

A harried man with a briefcase asked her how she was doing.

A guy with stacked empty cases of Pepsi on a dolly breezed past her, promising her that when he grew up his mom said he could get a real job.

Then she was alone.

And the fabric of the garage which was neutral and loose-knit just about any day, began to tighten around her like the filaments of a cocoon. She knew that anyone else standing there would not have felt it and that was because they were not *meant* to. This was for her. Like the card and the necklace, this was a private, almost intimate sort of horror that was being staged for her benefit and no other.

Okay, she thought, *bring out the white sheets and the drifting heads, rattle your fucking chains and make with the spooky groaning. Just do something.*

It began to build like a storm, the quality of the air becoming rarefied, electric with secret potential. Whatever in the hell it was, it was coming now. Her heart was beating fast and the skin from her pubis to her belly was crawling in prickly waves. The old tingling went up her back and settled at the nape of her neck like an icy fingernail had been drawn along her spine. And in her guts, there was that hot, fluttering sense of emptiness, of a vacancy waiting to be filled. It was complete, total, and unnerving. It was more than just a physical or psychological thing. Much deeper. Like her monthly period, she knew it was coming: an innate, organic, inborn, almost instinctual knowledge.

Terrifying in its erudition.

Then she heard the purr of a vehicle approaching. She was so utterly detached from ordinary sensation, that she was not even aware of the sound until it had built up around her with its immensity. It was not a big sound, but it was large, voluminous somehow.

And what rolled to a stop before her was not a delivery truck.

But a hearse.

The sight of it made her gasp, made her want to faint dead away. It was a big, black Cadillac, a huge and shiny beast from the 1950s and if it was a delusion, then it was a flawless one. It was long and wide with gleaming chrome S-shaped irons at the rear, purple-tinted cathedral windows hung with tasseled silver drapes and heavy velvet burgundy curtains drawn into arched billows.

And behind the wheel, the man with the pulpy, flyblown face.

He was smiling, his eyes glistening like tarnished nickels, the hole of his mouth revealing a soft and squirming darkness where his teeth should have been.

Christina teetered there on her feet. The window was rolled down and that man, that decaying thing, waved at her with one hideously distended hand. The inside of the hearse was full of flies. They were crawling over him, peppering the windshield. Their primal buzzing made her want to scream. A gassy, putrid stench was in her mouth and down her throat and up her nose and it was so bad she thought it would drag her guts up in moist coils, yank them from her mouth.

Time had gone rubbery.

Much like the contents of her stomach.

The driver's side door began to swing open slowly, creaking on its hinges like the lid of a casket. Christina uttered a wet, strangled sound in her throat and dropped to one knee, her head spinning, her skin crawling, her muscles gone limp and unresponsive.

She was looking down, down at the bottom of the door.

She saw one leg slide out, a pant leg threaded with mildew, a scuffed black shoe. Another leg followed it and then the pulpy man stood up and she heard a sloshing, squishing sound as his weight settled onto those rotting feet. Black juice squirted out the sides of his shoes like ink.

A few dead flies fell to his feet.

Christina would not look up. She would not see that face and the dank entombment it offered. She would not know that face, she would not let it haunt her dreams and waking moments and destroy all that she was. It was a crawling, insane pestilence and she would have none of it.

I will not look, it cannot make me look.

But she was wrong. She looked up and saw his ruined face, the collapsed channel of his nose, eyes that were black scabs. He grinned like a dead pike. The terror inside her incubated like an embryo as he held the squirming bundle in his arms out to her with genuine affection. It made a gurgling sound. Slowly, cradling the thing in the crook of one arm, he began to unwrap it, revealing the pulpous maggoty form beneath.

That's when she started to scream.

She turned, but did not rise. On all fours, she began crawling away from the hearse, loping along on hands and feet through the parking garage. Behind her, she could hear him following, but slowly and painfully, his feet making squishing sounds like rubber waders filled with mud and slime. The thing in his arms kept gurgling.

And that's how she escaped.

Crawling across the garage, eyes fixed and glassy, drool hanging from her mouth, a muted whimpering twisting in her throat. She was seen by others…a mad, gibbering thing more like a rat than a woman. There was something terribly absurd about a young woman in a skirted business suit scuttling about through a dirty garage like a sand spider.

And something fathomlessly terrifying.

7

She made it home and she had no memory of the journey, just some awful nightmarish images in her mind of crawling through graves and feeling moist clods of soil beneath her fingers. Sitting there on the floor of the kitchen, her eyes bovine and stunned, she sought out the only thing she could depend on which was the bottle of Absolut and began to drink.

By the time a pleasant little buzz had settled into her, making the tight coils inside her relax and her muscles unbind, she started thinking rationally again.

This is happening and you might as well accept it, she told herself. *So, with that in mind, are you going to deal with it or spend the rest of your days in a padded room with a mind like soft, warm putty?*

Dealing with it. She liked that. In horror movies, the characters sooner or later had to face what was terrorizing them. Maybe they died—usually they died—but they had to face up to it. The question was: did she have the guts for such a confrontation? She couldn't keep running and hiding and cowering. *But I don't have a choice. I'm not strong enough for something like this. I'm not a fighter. I've never been a fighter. I just want to hide.*

Which was true. She could get her ire up now and again, but she was by nature a mellow person who went with the flow which, she figured, was why her relationships always dead-ended sooner or later. It just wasn't in her to put her foot down when it needed putting down or to get her back up when trouble was heading her way. She was basically submissive. *A doormat,* a voice in her head reminded her. *People wipe their feet on you. They always have.*

"I have to do something," she said out loud.

But what?

What did sane people realistically do in situations like this? Maybe in movies they rose to the challenge...but in real life? In real life, she knew, they froze up with sheer terror, had a heart attack or a stroke, or they went to a therapist for volume antidepressant prescriptions.

That was what they did.

She sipped from her water glass of vodka, deciding that getting wasted probably wasn't the best course of action. And as she sipped, she remembered. Not only the corpse man, but what he held in his arms, because that was the very worst thing of all and the epicenter of her nightmare. *MOTHER, DEARLY BELOVED.* The memory of the locket and the dirt falling from it was the focal point of it all for her because it said everything that needed saying. In combination with the card and what the corpse man had said, it hinted at the most awful things.

But why her?

Was it simply at random? Simply because she'd happened to be in the cemetery at the wrong time and decided to tidy up that grave? Oh, the idea was silly, absurd, yet nothing else made sense. An act of kindness had drawn the attention of the corpse man and now he had selected her as mother to that vile little graveworm he carried.

There's got to be something to this, something I don't understand. A backstory or whatever you want to call it. It couldn't be this perfectly random.

She remembered what the corpse man held in his arms and how he had slowly unwrapped it for her like a sweet…God, it was some swollen, writhing sack with the most rudimentary of features, flat yellow eyes and reaching puffy hands. The memory of it made her shake so badly she had to set her glass down. Both dead. Both ghosts of a sort. The man looked like she expected a corpse to look…but the child…it looked barely human. Even putrefaction and the grave couldn't have distorted it that much. It looked more like some fleshy sentient tumor than a human being.

So kind. So caring. What a fine mother you shall be.

No, no way in hell would she be mother to that crawling horror. It would be a curse. An absolute curse that would shatter what was left of her mind.

Sitting there, she tried to think. She wasn't naïve enough to believe that this situation was just going to go away. It had to be dealt with. And in order to deal with it, she had to understand it. That made sense. But how did she go about it?

There was only one way.

Only one possible way and that was to go back to where it started: the cemetery. But not now. It was dark out.

8

The night boiled around her.

It lived and breathed and exhaled toxic vapors.

Black and grainy and ominously evil, it was silence and loneliness, sullen vacancy and the lack of it. A deep pool of mulling shadows where Christina suffocated, her eyes punched into purple-rimmed sightless circles, her mouth contorted and her fingers scratching senselessly into the inky, bloodless meat of midnight. She was drowning, sinking deeper into that nocturnal lagoon, her lungs saturated in a sweet blackness and she could smell the dank rot of coffins and buried things.

This was madness, a madness that was purely intimate…the sound of screams echoing from deserted houses in dead-end neighborhoods that reverberated in the cask of her skull.

Delirious and trembling, beyond the reach of vodka, she hid in her room in her little flat. Pressed between the bed and the cold plaster wall, she waited and breathed, her heart thudding and nerve endings jangling like wind chimes. She wanted to be smaller than she was, something thin and insubstantial that could steal under a bed or slide into a closet crack, cower beneath a thread of cobweb silk or sink into the floral jungle print of the wallpaper, never to be seen or touched or terrorized again.

She wanted a place that was her own.

A secret garden that was shaded and walled and utterly inviolate. And since no such place existed, she created one in her mind. A place reached through a see-sawing tangle of back alleys, gas-lit streets, and fog-shrouded courtyards. A place where she could hide and wait, while that cadaverous vulture forever circled, seeking an entrance that did not truly exist.

So, she cowered beneath the spreading umbrage of her secret, windowless garden, smelling the corpse man and feeling him and knowing him. A bleached and deathless thing, blown up with carrion-gases. Animated by lust and desire and a poisonous black heart that dared dream of love and tender intimacies, that conspired to touch and be touched. A hulking graveyard valentine. A gnawing, empty thing in search of a mother for its child.

Listen.

Christina.

No...no...no! That wasn't a voice, not really. It was only the slither of charnel worms and the buzz of gnawing corpse flies. The hiss of gaseous dissolution and the crackle of yellowed bones. Not a real voice, merely an echo, a shade, a ghost.

Christina...for thee, my love, have I prepared a place.

No, it was imagination. Not a grim face whose grimmer reflection swam across the surface of an antique looking glass. Not a creeping shadow on the stair. Not a creaking of the weather vane on the roof or white fingers scratching at a window pane.

Christina...in my ravening arms, thee I would embrace.

No! I am lost and you cannot find me. I'm too deep for your graveworms to burrow into or for your rats to chew. You'll not cover me in a mildewed shroud or press your bloated lips to my own. You will not drag me down into wedded tombs or make me lay on a bed of funeral lace. I will not squat at your fly-specked feet and mother that vermin you carry.

Christina, tender and kind, sweet of the sweet, blood of my blood and meat of my meat. The child hungers. It wishes to suckle—

Christina came up out of herself, carried on the discordant column of a scream. It yanked her up and out like rotting roots and tossed her into the world where love waited with a rictus corpse-grin and a churchyard devotion, a romance of cerements and sepulchers, wedding bouquets of dead roses and insect carapaces tossed like rice, the matrimonial requiems of exhumations and tolling death bells, and a squirming grub waited to suckle its mother.

She came up out of herself, gasping and drumming her hands on the floor, knowing the corpse man was near and knowing he would find her and take her as his own for he needed love and a mother for his child.

Listen.

Yes, a groaning, a creaking of bridles and bits, the clopping of horse's hooves. The whisper of satin and the rasp of leather. The clank of chains and the death-rattle of hollow oblong boxes. The strident scratchings of low-key funereal violins. The stench of grave orchids and fresh black earth.

She clambered to her feet and stumbled to the window, staring down not at the city, but maybe at a memory of the city four or five generations gone. Tall, narrow buildings like obelisks and tombstones flanking a misty cobbled street. And down that street, a glass-sided, gilt-edged funeral coach pulled by black, velvet-covered horses. Pallbearers and mourners in silk-banded top hats and matching gloves marched alongside. And sitting atop the coach, beneath a nodding plume of ostrich feathers, was the corpse man in a lavender suit, stovepipe hat balanced atop his collapsing head.

Christina screamed.

A funeral coach was coming to collect her so she could be taken away to the marriage vault, fitted with a cerecloth bridal gown still moldered and stained from its previous owner. Drawn up an altar of black crepe, the eyeless cemetery faces of the dearly beloved flickering yellow from the guttering flames of tall, dripping funereal tapers. They would sit on crumbling earthen boxes, skeletal hands folded on cobwebbed laps. Confetti and yellow paper bells would be suspended over water-stained cement block walls thick with grave fungus. And screaming, her mind gone to a soft, oozing mush, Christina would be carried over a threshold of bones and laid out in the ruffled satin confines of the marriage bed, head pressed down upon a satin pillow as her husband lay down atop her, rotting face and wormy lips pressed to her own.

First a bride, then a mother.

She stumbled away from the window, knowing what she had seen was one part lunacy and one part premonition tightening around her mind like a hemp noose.

She almost made it to the bed before she went out cold. But even then, she wasn't alone.

9

A pounding.
     A hammering.
Horses' hooves? Shovels patting down the earth above her dripping, dank marriage box? Or was it the sound of her own fists forever thudding against a weighted lid that would never open?

Christina came awake in the sunshine, breathing hard, fingers clawing at the carpeting beneath her. She could not remember where she was or how she had come to be there. Nothing made sense. Her body ached. Everything was sore no matter which way she moved. She looked around, the world taking on substance before her. She was in her apartment. She kept telling herself that...yet the stench of rifled graves and dark soil remained.

Still, the pounding.

Someone had come to exhume her, to free her from this oblong box.

Stop it! You're not in a box!

The pounding went on and on.

She thought: *It can't be him, it cannot be him...not here and not now...not in the sunshine like this...*

But that was when he had first come courting, was it not? In the brightness and sunshine, the middle of a high summer afternoon. Christina waited, worried, trying to remember where she had been. All she could recall was work. Nancy had slept over and they'd gone to work and it had been a normal day and...and...

Lunchtime.

The hearse.

The dead man.

Yes, she had been on the run since, mostly in her mind, trying to stay afloat in a raging sea of hysteria. Dear God, what had happened? What had she been doing? She looked down at her skirt and blouse. They were filthy. They looked like they'd been used to wipe out an urn. Her fingers were mottled with grime, dirt caught beneath her fingernails.

More pounding.

Now a jangling of keys.

She could hear Nancy's voice out there. The landlord griping. Another voice. A man talking in low tones. The three of them discussing things. Christina knew then that Nancy had brought the police. She would not have stood still for Christina not showing up from the lunch run. She would have searched all day and night. She was a force of nature, once roused. And now she had brought the authorities.

But would those be the police or the nice young men in their clean white coats?

She ran off to her bedroom, frantically stripping off her dirty clothes, throwing on a robe and running a washcloth over her face. In the mirror, it was sallow and pinched, brown crescent moons stained beneath the eyes, lower lip trembling...was that her face? Dear God, it looked wizened and mad, the hair just touched with gray.

What have I been doing and who have I been doing it with?

Nancy came in first, followed by a bespectacled man with thinning sandy hair that she had never seen before. Last was Frazer, the landlord. He looked dour and crabby as usual, his single bushy gray eyebrow arching like the back of a caterpillar. He looked like he wanted to say something to Christina, something about how he didn't care for this kind of business and maybe he should have known that she was an odd-duck the first time he laid eyes on her, Jesus H. Christ, Lord love a duck. But he looked into her eyes which were like smoldering quicksilver and he changed his mind, leaving quickly.

"Christina?" Nancy said. She didn't look too good herself, circles under her eyes, worry lines at the corners of her mouth. "Where in the hell have you been? I've been calling here all night...what's going on?"

Christina sighed. "I've been sleeping. I turned the phone off."

But Nancy wasn't having that. It looked very much like she was ready for a tirade, but she checked herself, threw whatever was simmering in her head onto the back burner. For now, anyway. No sense getting pissed-off and emotional in front of this stranger. "All right, Christy," she said. "Now, why don't you tell me why you never came back from the lunch run?"

"I felt weak, dizzy...I came home and laid down. I just woke up." She turned towards the man. "And who are you? A psychiatrist?"

"Close. I'm a cop. Mark Crews, Missing Persons."

Christina almost giggled. A cop? He sure didn't look like a cop. He wore a nice tailored suit, was freshly-scrubbed and soft-spoken. Round and pink-cheeked, he looked like a CPA, if anything. She just couldn't imagine this inoffensive man running down crooks.

"You look like shit," Nancy said.

"I feel like shit."

Nancy stood there a moment, then sat on the couch with Crews. "You were dizzy and not feeling well, eh? I see, I see. Well, you should have called. You really missed all the excitement. See, a bunch of people down in the parking garage saw some crazy bitch crawling around on her hands and knees like a shit beetle. They kept saying how she looked like you." She dismissed that with a wave of her hand. "But that's crazy, right? My friend Christina wouldn't do that. No way. Because if something happened, if she was threatened or scared, she would have come straight to me because she knows I would help her."

Christina narrowed her eyes, remembering. Yes, yes, the hearse, then the panic attack, crawling out of there, sliding under cars, making for the stairs. Loping down them like an ape and running the six blocks to her apartment. She remembered now, surprised she had not been arrested and confined.

Are you sure you ran straight back here? Wasn't there something else? Something you're trying desperately not to remember? Something about a ride in an antique hearse? She swallowed, beginning to tremble. Yes, something had happened. Something terrible. All the dirt on her…she had gone somewhere else, been taken to another undisclosed location to spend time with—

"Christina?" Nancy said. "Are you with us here?"

"Yes, yes."

"Could have fooled me. You're tuning in and tuning out like an old radio and…" Nancy leaned closer, wrinkling her nose. "…and you smell like a fifth of rotgut."

Crews just sat there watching the exchange.

Nancy folded her arms across her chest. "You saw *him* didn't you? That fucking ghost?"

Christina saw no point in lying. The cop would have her in a rubber room before long. Might as well make his job easier. "Yes, I saw him. He pulled into the garage in this garish, ugly-old hearse. Quite a ride. He was all bloated-up and white and full of flies. He had the baby with him. It looked like a plump graveworm. Anything else you need to know?"

Nancy looked scared. "Then…then you ran?"

"Yes, I ran. I hid here." Christina stifled a giggle with her hand. "At least, I think I did. I woke up on the floor a few minutes before you showed. I had weird dreams. Can't remember 'em real good. Something about caskets and mausoleums. You know what's funny, though? What's really funny?"

Nancy and Crews were staring at her like something was going to happen, like maybe she was a Jack-in-the-Box that had been wound too tight and any second now she'd come springing up, her head flying off and bouncing against the ceiling.

"What's really funny," she said, "is that I was still dressed in my good clothes from work and they were all dirty like I'd been rolling around in the dirt...or maybe in an open grave."

She held out her hands so they could see the ground-in dirt.

They looked at each other and looked away.

She smiled. "Thanks for coming, Mr. Crews, but I'm afraid the police can't do much on this one."

"I'm not just here as a cop, Christy. I'm a friend of Nancy's. I want to help." He stood up. "Let me just run through this. You went to your mother's grave and saw some sort of apparition, right? Then the card came, the necklace. And now an antique hearse pulled up in the parking garage at your work? You can't remember what happened after that?"

Christina nodded. "That about sums it up. When do the men with nets come to collect me?"

"They don't use nets anymore. Too expensive." He smiled thinly, almost apologetically. "I don't think you're nuts, Christy. I honestly don't know what's going on, but I'd like to help you."

"Why?"

"Why? Well, because Nancy is my friend and you're hers. That's good enough for a start. And if you need more than that, let's just say I spend all day behind a desk trying to track down people who don't want to be found and once, just once, I'd like to sink my teeth into something tangible."

Christina didn't know what to say, so she chuckled dryly. *"Tangible?* Mister, you got off at the wrong stop. This is a ghost story, there's nothing tangible about it."

"Can I see your hands?" he asked.

Christina held them out and Crews examined them. "You have very lovely hands, Christy. Long fingers, fine-boned."

She snatched them back, looked over at Nancy like she wanted to know what kind of fetishist this guy was.

"What do you think?" Nancy said to him.

He shook his head. "Too small, fingers too thin. Could have smeared, I guess."

"What the hell are you two talking about?" Christina demanded.

Nancy looked over at her. "Honey, there's dirty handprints all over the outside of your door...like somebody was slapping their hands out there, trying to get in."

Christina was scared, but not surprised. "And you thought maybe I did it? That maybe I'm just crazy and inventing all this shit, rigging a few clues to support my own fucked-up agenda?"

Crews looked at her, his eyes very soft and his face very kind. "Listen, Christy...if you were us and heard these things, what would you do?"

She laughed with a bitter, metallic sound. "I'd have me committed before I hurt someone. That's what I'd do."

"Christy, please," Nancy said.

Christina pitied her. In fact, she pitied both of them because they were naïve enough to be pitying *her*. They didn't understand. They *couldn't* understand. It was all beyond human comprehension. They were suspicious of the entire situation, their common sense telling them that she was on the verge of a breakdown or possibly even well past one. What they needed was evidence.

So she gave them some.

"You must feel like you totally wasted your time, Mr. Crews. I feel bad about that so I'm going to make things worth your while." She loosened the belt of her robe, then pulled it open so her bare breasts were on full display. "Take a close look, a very close look."

"Christy!" Nancy said in shock.

Crews' mouth was hanging open.

They both soon got over it, though, as they examined the circular red welts on her breasts and the bruised indents from teeth.

As a tear ran down one cheek, Christina said, "Go ahead. Touch them so you know the bites are real, that I didn't fake this, too." She gauged the looks on their faces as being a combination of awe and terror. "And, just so you know, I'm not a contortionist so that should eliminate the idea that I bit them myself."

Nancy and Crews looked from her breasts to each other. It was very clear they didn't know what to say.

"Any other questions? Good. Now, if you'll excuse me, I need a shower."

10

Two quiet days.

Two empty days.

Two days of unknown longings and secret desires that were not Christina's at all, but those of something deathless and decayed that had invaded not only her reality, but her dreams. She was a host, she decided. A host for the parasite the corpse man wanted her to mother over, something that had crawled up from the black sewer of the universe to drain her soul dry one drop at a time. And she knew, knew very well, that it didn't honestly matter how much love and attention Nancy poured on her or how many cops she brought into this…what was slated to happen was going to happen. And it would not be for them. This perversity would not allow them to interfere, for this was too intimate for the company of strangers.

This was a matter of a corpse and his bride…and their child.

The knowledge of that brought a sickness down upon her, one that was hot and cold and wasting. An infection of mind and body that pushed her into bed and held her there with cold hands slick and greasy with the drainage of tumors and plague-boils. She coughed and sweated, shook and vomited, and finally went still, adrift in a steaming sea of fevers. She could see the walls of her room and the ceiling, the secret patterns therein. She sucked in lungfuls of hot, stale air and let them back out again. Felt her heart pounding, inflating with blood and withering back down from the lack of it. She was here, in the bed, and somewhere else, maybe nowhere discernable or perhaps just wedged between this place and another. Her hands bunched into fists, fell into the bedclothes like dead moths…white and limp.

And then Nancy came out of the fog, saying, "You still look like shit, but I think you might live."

Christina breathed. "Really?"

"Yes, that's my unqualified medical opinion."

"How long? How long have I been laying here?"

Nancy smiled. "How long does it seem?"

"Either ten minutes or two weeks. You decide."

"Nearly twenty-four hours."

Nancy held her hand and told her there was nothing to worry about. She had taken care of everything at the office and taken in the mail, looked after things that needed looking after. "So you see, everything's fine."

And Christina wanted to tell her how very wrong she was, how she could never truly understand the depths of this particular nightmare, but there were no words that could frame what she felt and what she'd seen and what was even then creeping out of the spectral darkness to claim her. And if there were words, there was certainly no strength to link them into chains that would make sense. So, Christina said nothing and asked nothing. She did not want to know what was going on in the world, for what was going on outside of it was plenty for what remained of her mind. She wanted Nancy to climb into bed with her, to press herself against her and hold her tight, so tightly that the corpse man would never, ever be able to wrest her free. Maybe together they could beat this awfulness, this disease of the soul, together as one. But Nancy would misconstrue that, she would think there was something sexual implied while there certainly was not. It was funny how the ingrained mores of society clung even in such deranged times. Christina would have laughed if she could have. Maybe Nancy would be offended and maybe she would be delighted and maybe repulsed at the idea of pressing her flesh against Christina's own which was lit with the tomb-glow of fevers.

I won't put her in that position, I won't put anyone in that position. I'll take what's been willed to me.

And thinking that way frightened her, because that was the logic of acceptance. No more denial, no more fighting, just take whatever nameless horror fate had selected for her, take it into her arms and embrace it as her mind went to a cold, bubbling sludge.

Nancy said she was staying the night again and Christina told her that was ridiculous, that she was better now. The sickness and hysteria were gone. But Nancy just laughed and told her she wasn't much of a liar.

Then Christina slipped away or maybe she was already gone. No matter, for her eyes would not open and she could only see those old buildings again and that cobbled road hung with a wreath of mist. The funeral wagon. Men with tall, narrow top hats and antique suits carrying coffin-shaped wicker creels out of doorways and inside those baskets, Christina could hear the dead scratching, the dead mourning themselves, the dead speaking in shattered, insane voices of love and sensation as if death had torn away their minds.

And then she was behind that horse-drawn hearse, smelling dead flowers and grave-mists, an overpowering stench of waterlogged things rotting away in pine boxes. The door to the rear of the wagon was open and there was the corpse man, crouched amongst a litter pile of caskets. His face was a grotesque aberration, not flesh but white wax that had pooled in irregular mounds and ruts, knobs and hollows. His eyes were dirty copper. He was chewing on a human femur, nibbling and slobbering it with passionate kisses, working it like a child with a candy cane, sucking and licking out the globs of creamy white marrow until the bone was emptied like a straw. And then he began to blow over the open end of the bone as if it were an empty bottle, making a haunting and melancholy tune that made something run inside of Christina. It was a tune, she knew, that was played on battlefields of old, in country churchyards at dusk to ease the dead into the next world.

A dirge.

And it held her in that dream-life, possessing her and making her believe that such an undead and pure sort of love could not possibly be a bad thing. She kept thinking this as she drifted with the dank fog at the back of the hearse, feeling dark shrouds falling over her like woolen blankets, wrapping her up like Sunday afternoons

And maybe she would have crossed the altar then, but the corpse man stopped playing that beautiful hymn, that timeless ode to those fallen and entombed and kissed of the conquering worm. He pulled the femur from his bloating lips and said, *"My darling, my darling, my love of tomorrow promised to me so many yesterdays gone..."*

Then he had the bundle in his arms, holding it out to her and she saw the thing inside, quivering and undulant, a seamed leathery bag with thin pulsing black veins just under the skin. It grinned with a crooked slash of mouth, its eyes like yellow seeds. It pursed its lips, making sucking sounds.

And Christina came awake.

The scream that came from her lips was perfectly silent and perfectly insane.

11

When Nancy finally left and went to work, Christina breathed a sigh of relief. Nancy was great. She was the best friend anyone could hope to have, but the motherly devotion wore thin after a while and as much as Christina appreciated it, she wasn't a child. Things needed doing and she couldn't do them with Nancy hanging around.

She took a hot shower and fixed herself up, threw on a pair of joggers and a V-neck Tee and drove out to the cemetery. What she didn't do was let fear rule her. Down deep, of course, she was terrified but she knew she had to get beyond that if she was going to figure this out. So she pulled into the cemetery and parked where she had last time.

It was a nice day, sunny and warm. The flowers were blooming and the air smelled of fresh-cut grass. She sat there in the car with the windows open, smelling summer and feeling it, breathing it in. If she hadn't been parked on a road in a cemetery, she might have been able to fool herself that this was a beautiful day in the country. But, of course, she knew better.

Once she had pumped up her resolve, she stepped out and walked in the direction of her mother's grave. At that moment, she felt oddly strong and oddly resolute, two things she had never been and especially of late. In the back of her mind, she knew she was forcing a meeting with the corpse man here in the direct rays of sunlight as it had been that first day. Maybe he owned the darkness, but she wanted to believe that the daylight hours were hers...even if he had already routinely shown twice in the afternoon.

When she got to her mother's grave, she looked down at it with rising cynicism, thinking, *well, you wanted me to have a husband and child, didn't you?* In her head, there was sardonic laughter.

She moved on.

Here was the grave she had so innocently tended that day, pulling weeds and thinking she was doing a fine, selfless thing only to discover that the road to hell was most surely paved with good intentions and that no good deed went unpunished. Sighing, she looked down at the leaning gray headstone.

CHARLES DAVID SLICK
1907—1956
BELOVED SON

"Beloved?" she said under her breath. "How about *accursed?*"

She thought she felt something around her when she said that, a stirring of the air, a cold and clammy current going up her spine. She was not afraid. She had been through far too much by that point to get the heebie-jeebies so easily. If anything, she felt angry. She looked around to see if the corpse man had sprouted like an oily, morbid mushroom but he had not.

"Guess what, Charles David fucking Slick? You make me sick. Guess what again? I don't really like children and I never have. I don't have any because God knew a neurotic wreck when he saw one and he wasn't about to saddle a kid with a headcase like me." She paused, feeling good, really good. "So if you're looking for a mother for that maggot in your arms, look somewhere else."

She looked around again, filled with herself now, almost daring him to show so she could tear him apart with her bare hands. But he did not show.

"Well?" she said. "C'mon already! Show! Crawl up out of your grave or slither on out of hell! *You heard me! Show yourself! C'MON YOU GUTLESS CRAWLING FUCKING SHITWORM, SHOW YOURSELF!*"

She realized she had not only raised her voice, but she was actually shouting, practically screaming. A couple of old ladies in the distance were staring in her direction. When she met their gaze, they hurried off.

"Yeah? Well, fuck all of you," Christina said, aiming a kick at the tombstone and connecting with great force. She didn't think anything would happen but she was wrong. The stone was old and leaning. It fell right over and cracked in half upon impact. In the back of her mind she thought she heard a dozen voices sighing.

"There's no reason for that."

She spun around, caught between cold white fear and violent primal aggression. Frank Betts was standing there, looking much as he had that first day in green work pants and cap, huge hands on his hips, sad eyes like melting butter in his rugged sunburned face.

"I...I didn't think anything would happen."

Frank nodded, lighting a cigarette but saying nothing as clouds of blue smoke danced away on the breeze. Christina took his silence as a sign of indignation and said, "I'll pay for it, okay? Just send me a bill. I'll pay whatever it costs."

He shrugged. "I'm guessing you had a reason and I'm guessing that reason is not good."

"You know something, don't you?"

"About what?"

Her eyes narrowed. "About this grave and the person who is supposed to be under it."

"I know some rumors and hearsay. I know that women who've tended that grave out of generosity sometimes have...problems later on."

"Hauntings, you mean?"

He shrugged again. "If you get back on the county road and head into town you'll see a white church on your right and if you turn down that old road you'll see a lot of big old houses, many of which have fallen to ruin and many others that have been broken up into apartments."

"And what does that have to do with anything?"

"You'll see a little ranch house on the corner of Everest and Pine. You'll notice it don't belong there amongst those Victorian monstrosities, a little squat post-World War II house like that, and you'll be right in your thinking. See, the original house—belonged to a clan named Slick—burned down back in the 1950s. Sad, sad affair. Still, there were many back then that thought it was for the best, all things considered."

"And why was that?"

Frank lit another cigarette, staring out across the fields of monuments. "Anyway, after that big old barn burned to the ground," he said, ignoring her question, "the family, those still living, built that ranch there. A practical, Spartan sort of house in great contrast to what stood there before. These days, you might be interested to know, there's still a Slick living there. Harriet. Folks call her Hattie. She's the niece of Charles David. She'd be well into her seventies by now but she knows all the family secrets. If you were to knock on the door and ask some questions about her kin, she'll tell you to get the hell off her property. She's one evil twat. And I make no excuse for using that word in connection with Hattie. But don't take any shit. She's got a mouth on her like a sailor, but she's old and frail. You're young and strong. Barge your way in there and demand to be told about her uncle."

"What do you know about him?"

Frank shrugged. "He was an odd duck, I'll tell you that much. He was an undertaker, too. I guess they'd call it a funeral director or some such crap now. Back then, we called them undertakers. He worked for some big outfit in the city. I grew up in that neighborhood and nobody much cared for him when he came to stay with Hattie's mom and her people. I don't think it was because of what he did for a living but more that he was just a real strange fellow. A weirdo."

Frank told her that Charles David was very lonely. No friends, no girls in his life. He'd tried to date just about every single woman in the neighborhood, but they didn't want anything to do with him.

"A real romantic, I guess. He'd send them flowers but everyone joked that they were funeral flowers. People could be heartless then as they can be now."

"And?"

"And what?"

"There's something you're not saying."

"If there is, it can wait until after you talk to Hattie."

With that, Frank Betts turned on his heels, cutting between a family mausoleum and a clustered pod of headstones. Only when he was well away from the Slick grave did he start whistling.

Christina watched him leave, wondering if she had the guts to take on Hattie.

12

The house was easy to find. Like Frank said it didn't really seem to belong amongst the sad old Victorians, the majority of which had seen better days. The ranch was plain, boxy, sitting dead center of a yard with huge elm trees rising up into the sky that pretty much dwarfed it. In her mind, Christina could just about imagine what it must have looked like here on the corner before the fire: that tall narrow house shuttered and dark, architecturally insane, towers and spires, a Charles Addams sort of place much as the family that lived within its walls.

But now...well, the ranch was like an eyesore amidst the fading grandeur of the rows of historical homes. It was vinyl-sided, glaring white with black trim. There were even gaudy yellow plastic sunflowers spinning in the breeze surrounded by an assortment of garden gnomes and thermoformed bunnies and ducks. *Tacky* wasn't strong enough of a word for it.

She hopped out and went up the walk before she lost her nerve. She rang the doorbell three times before a voice screeched from inside, *"What the hell do you want?"*

The screen door was open and Christina stepped into a neat little house with prints of sad clowns on the walls. It smelled like bacon grease and cat piss in there. "I'm looking for Harriet Slick," she called out.

A figure lumbered through an archway that must have led into the kitchen. "Well, you've found her."

Hattie Slick was an immense, fleshy woman, slug-like, face wrinkled and pouched by fat, mouth toothless, lips blue-tinged as if they were oxygen-starved. She wore a drab yellow sort of housecoat with abundant food stains on it. She studied her uninvited guest with rheumy eyes set in puffy, narrowing sockets. In one arm was a bowl of what looked like macaroni-and-cheese cradled to the heavy spillage of one breast. Her other hand—dry, scabby, and claw-like—held a wooden mixing spoon. "Now I ask you again, what the hell do you want?"

"My name is Christina Fortenay. I need to talk to you about a relation of yours."

"All my relations are dead."

"I want to talk about your uncle. His name was Charles David Slick."

Hattie shook her head from side to side. She had looked old and weary when she first came out of the kitchen, but now she looked ready for the grave. "I...I'm not in the habit of discussing family business with just any hot young tart who forces her way into my home, so get out of here."

"But it's important."

Hattie set the bowl of mac-and-cheese on a chair. "Is it now? I bet everything in your life is important, little miss pissy. I bet it's *urgent*. I bet you think the world revolves around your sweet little ass but you're wrong! *You...are...wrong, Missy!* Dead wrong in this house. So go away! Scat! I didn't invite you here and I don't know who the hell you think you are barging into my house! I'm not about to wake the dead and drag their dirty secrets out just because you say so! So piss off."

Christina stood her ground. It was 100% unlike her because she really had never stood her ground in her entire life as a wallflower. Now and again she got her dander up (like when she kicked Uncle Charlie's headstone over), but it was of rare occurrence...yet, here she was not backing down. When she spoke, she spoke calmly but with an edge to her voice. "I want to know about Charles David and I'm not leaving until I do."

She expected Hattie to start screaming and raving, threatening to call the police and have her jailed and sued...but that's not what the old woman did. Like a child that was scolded, she walked uneasily into the living room. She was speaking even before Christina got in there. The funny thing was that she didn't seem to be speaking to her, but the blank face of the TV that was turned off or didn't work in the first place.

"...and he came from bad stock like all the Slicks and what came to take possession of him was something terrible handed down the family line. I was just a teenager but I remember the gossip and the dirty skeletons in the family closet and all that stuff they tried to keep from me. But why does that matter? Uncle Charles came here to live with us and he was in his twenties, I guess, a strange sort, and he lived upstairs at the back of the house and he barely came down for meals or anything else. I can see him now...real pale and dark-eyed. You always got the feeling that he was seeing things in a room you were not. I didn't like him. Nobody liked him, but he was family. That probably means nothing to a little strumpet like you, but there was a day when such things meant the world."

She kept talking and Christina listened to her voice shrilling and scratching like a bow scraped over an out-of-tune fiddle. She went on in great detail about the importance of family, trying to drive home that very point, overcompensating as if she didn't really believe it herself. Christina listened and her head ached and she was struck by the unpleasant realization that Hattie's voice was very similar to that of her mother and they were both filled with wrath and venom. *Don't you know enough to leave this poor woman alone? Don't you have better sense than that, Chrissy? Didn't I raise you up any better? Can't you see how this woman has suffered and how that suffering is centered out at the cemetery in that grave you foolishly decided to tend? She's got secrets buried in there and here you are, trying to pry them out of her! Shame on you! If you had a man in your life and a home to keep and children to mind, you wouldn't be such a little nosy, prying little—*

"How did he die?" Christina said, mostly to knock that shrewish voice from her head.

"Maybe there are things I'll talk of and those I won't," Hattie said, plugging a Benson & Hedges 120 into her puckered mouth and lighting up. Her hand shook as she did so.

Bullshit, Christina thought. *You've been waiting for years for a chance to vent all this and we both know it. I couldn't shut you up if I wanted to.*

"I need to know how he died."

The cigarette gave Hattie strength. "And why would that be any of your business?" she wanted to know. The cigarette had given her back some of her ire, but not as much as she liked to pretend because just under it, Christina could sense a shriveling, naked fear. She needed to say things but she was almost afraid to. "Why would any of this be your business? You barge into my house, start sticking your nose into my family's private affairs, and you never tell me *why* you have to know so damn desperately. That probably works for you just fine out there, Missy. You wiggle your ass and shake your tits and the boys do whatever you say. But it doesn't buy you beans here. IT DOES NOT BUY YOU GODDAMN BEANS!"

The way she said it, shouting the last part, it was as if there was someone else in the house and she wanted them to hear. Maybe that was part of it. Maybe she wanted to tell, *needed* to tell even, but some part of her didn't want it to be her idea. As if it was okay if it was coerced out of her.

"You're going to tell me," Christina said, sounding firm and playing the game. "I won't leave until I know."

Hattie pulled off her cigarette. Her entire body was trembling now, not just her hands. "You're going to kill me! That's what you're going to do! You're going to make me say things I shouldn't say and it'll be the end of me! The absolute end of me. You want me to die! You want awful things to happen to me!"

Christina was having trouble keeping up with Hattie's shifting emotions, but she knew it was part of the game. For her own benefit, she was acting as if she had no choice in the matter. It was being dragged out of her even at the cost of her own life.

And why was that? Because she thought Uncle Charles was listening?

"Tell me," Christina demanded.

Hattie set her cigarette in a nearby ashtray. It seemed as if she was gasping for breath. Her face had gone red as a ripe tomato and there were tears in her eyes. "You don't know what you're starting. You just don't know."

"Yes, I do. I was there. At the cemetery. I was visiting my mother. I picked the weeds from your uncle's headstone and then—"

"No! No! *No!*" she stammered. "I don't want to know about this! I don't want to hear it! Can't you see that I've been through enough? *Can't you see that?*"

Christina saw that, but she didn't care. She had to know. Even if Hattie Slick pitched over dead from a heart attack, she could not stop pressing her because it was beyond the point of being sympathetic now.

Hattie picked up her cigarette and took a few rapid puffs off it. "He died in the old house. The one that burned down. It sat right here, right on this spot, a long time ago. He died because of things that were happening. He was too afraid to live and when he died, we were happy because it was for the best. The men...they went up there and found him. That's what I was told. That very day, the house burned."

"He committed suicide?"

"Yes. Yes, that's what he did."

But there was more to it than that and Christina knew it. There were plenty of suicides in the world and she highly doubted they all came back as ghosts or shades or revenants or whatever you wanted to call them. This situation was special. It was unique. It was powerful enough to drag him out of his grave and she needed to know why.

"Why did he do it?"

"I told you, he was afraid."

"Afraid to live?"

"That, too, sure."

This was going nowhere. She would have to try a different approach. "Okay. So the men went up there and found him...but nobody else?"

Hattie shook her head. "I was just a kid! I wasn't allowed to look on something like that!"

"So you didn't go up there?"

"I told you that, didn't I?"

Yes, she had told her that but Christina didn't believe her. She was lying. It was all over her liver-spotted face and in the depths of her dark eyes.

"What did you see?"

Hattie shook her head back and forth. "I told you, I didn't even—"

"What did you see?"

Hattie began to sob uncontrollably as she opened doors in the back of her mind that had been shut a long, long time. She sat there, shaking, the cigarette trembling in her lips, the ash nearly two inches long. Her face was sallow and wrinkled, wet with tears. "They were...they were getting everybody out of the house. They said there was a fire. But that wasn't true and I knew it wasn't true. I didn't smell any smoke. No, there wasn't a fire...but you could bet there was *going* to be. While they tried to get everyone outside, I slipped up the stairs. I had to see. I had to know..."

The house was alive with people shouting and screaming, so Hattie took advantage of that and snuck upstairs. She crept to the doorway that led to the attic room and, her heart pounding away in her chest, she took those stairs up, one by one. The fifth one creaked and she avoided it. The stairwell was narrow. Her shoulders nearly brushed the walls. This was where Uncle Charles lived. Up there. Up in the attic room and she had never, ever dared to go up there. Not before and especially not after horrible things happened in the neighborhood and people were saying the most terrible things about him. But there she was, creeping like a mouse up the stairs and the door above got closer and she could see that it was ajar and there was a tongue of yellow light coming out from under it.

"By the time I reached that door," Hattie said, her words trembling on her tongue, her eyes wide and unblinking, "I was so scared...God, I was so scared. I could barely get enough wind if my lungs to breathe. I was dizzy. I was quivering. It felt like my stomach was in the back of my throat. I reached out for the doorknob and I barely had the strength to open it…"

But she did open it, oh yes.

She opened it and stood there on the threshold reeling with building anxiety. There was a lantern, a gas lantern, on the floor before the doorway. Its light was bright and yellow and it threw long, crawling ebon shadows over the walls and the vaulted ceiling that were like slinking black cats. She saw the bed, highboy, and dresser about a split second before she saw Uncle Charles.

He was drifting two feet off the floor like a ghost that had come in the night to suck her blood…but that was only because there was a rope around his neck that was tied off to an open beam above. He was naked and there was a stool overturned beneath him. He was white and tumescent like a dead fish, his knees touching, his fingers splayed. His skin was of a smooth, even whiteness, in great contrast to his face which was purple-blue like a great bruise going black with infection. His tongue hung between his lips like a flap, his neck crooked, the bone pushing out through the side like the stub of a broomstick.

And that was bad…dear God, it was horrendous…but the very worst thing was that she could clearly see that something had been at him. His bloodless, porcelain flesh was scratched and scraped, his belly and thighs set with bite marks.

"That's what I saw. That's exactly what I saw," Hattie said, her voice laced tight with terror, the tone no longer scratching but high-pitched and childlike. "He was hanging above me and there was a sort of sunken grin on his lips and I guess I was afraid he was going to open his eyes. That's when I screamed."

Christina swallowed. "I imagine it must have been…traumatizing."

Hattie shook her head. "It wasn't that corpse hanging there that made me scream. No…it was that thing *squatting* in the corner, that twisted-up little shape that was afraid to come out into the light. The one that was staring at me with shining yellow eyes."

13

When the knock came at the door, Nancy nearly leaped from her chair and threw it open. Mark Crews was standing there.

"Please tell me nothing has happened to her," she said.

"Nothing has. At least, nothing I know about."

"Of course nothing has," Nancy said, knowing she was going overboard but some part of her—some very desperate part—was worrying that she wasn't going overboard quite enough. Christina meant the world to her. She was her best friend. Good God, she was her *only* friend when you came down to it. At least, the only one that mattered.

She saw how Mark was looking at her. There was great sympathy in his eyes and she knew he wanted to put his arms around her. But she wasn't going to allow that. Not now. She was not about to become the simpering, weak-kneed female that needed a man's strong arms around her...even if, at that moment, she thought such a thing would be very nice.

"So tell me what happened," he said.

Nancy sat on the couch by him. "I don't know. Nothing probably." She sighed. "I've been keeping an eye on her with everything that's been going on."

"And?"

"And I left for work. I didn't like leaving her alone, you know, but things are piling up on my desk. I had to go. Around ten, I got a real bad feeling so I called her. No answer. I came here and she was gone."

"And?"

"What do mean, *and?*"

It was his turn to sigh. "Nancy, I think Christina has enough going on without you panicking. Has it ever occurred to you that she went for a walk or is out shopping? Maybe she had to pick up a prescription. Maybe she went to the bank or out for a cheeseburger. It's been known to happen."

Instead of going off on him, which would have been her normal reaction...she simply smiled. It was a painted-on smile and about as real as a stuffed mermaid, but at least she made the attempt. "Yes, it's been known to happen. But I've been here, Mark. I've been at ground zero when most of this Stephen King fucking shit has been happening to her. I know damn well the last thing on her mind is a walk in the park or buying a new pair of jeans or a foot-long Coney and cheese fries."

"Has there been...?"

"No, nothing. At least, nothing I know of, thank God. She spent a good day or so in bed with the fevers. Shaking and crying out with nightmares. I was by her side the entire time."

"But nothing...unexplainable?"

"No."

"No more bites?"

Nancy's eyes narrowed. "I don't spend a lot of time looking at her tits, Mark."

But the sly look in his eyes told her that he was not entirely convinced of that. He studied his hands, the carpeting, the coffee table.

"What?" Nancy said. "What are you thinking?"

"I'm thinking about the bites."

And Nancy nearly said, *No, you're thinking about her tits.* Of course, she didn't. That would have been wrong, out of place, a jealous sort of reaction. But he was male and Christina was a pretty girl and *yes*, her tits were delightful. Why wouldn't he be thinking about them? Sometimes, Nancy thought about them herself. Yet, the idea of Mark thinking of them made her burn inside...and was that because she had a thing for her best friend or was it because Mark was noticing Christina more than her?

"Which interests you more," she asked before she could stop herself, "her tits or the bites?"

"As a cop or a man?"

"I'm sorry. I don't know why I said that."

But she did. Deep down she was worried that Mark and Christina would hook up and she would be out of the picture entirely. That bothered her and what bothered her even more was that he was thinking things like that.

Mark, knowing Nancy as he did, said, "Let's clear the air, shall we? Yes, your friend is attractive and, yes, her breasts are very nice. You can tell her I said both of those things. I have no shame. Maybe it'll make her feel better about herself."

"And it would definitely make you feel better if she was in your bed."

"Enough, Nancy. I'm kidding."

"I know. I'm stressed. When I get like this my mind can't keep up with my mouth." She laughed thinly. "If I told her you said that she'd crawl under her bed. You don't know her. She gets like that."

"She doesn't like compliments?"

"No, they make her squirm."

"See, I thought all women liked compliments."

"Shows what you know."

He laughed. "Before we go on, just so you know, I have no designs on your friend. You know damn well I've been trying to get you in bed for two years. I won't risk your delights over Christina."

"You asshole," Nancy said, but she laughed, she really laughed and she felt better inside where it counted. Something felt less threatened and something else felt oddly vindicated.

"But back to Christina's bite marks—and I think we can both be sure that they *are* bite marks. You called me over here as a friend and as a cop. So, now comes the cop part. I'm going to ask you a few questions and they're going to be hard questions, but I don't have a choice." He cleared his throat, ratcheting himself into cop mode. "I don't believe in ghosts, Nancy, and I don't think you do either. So let's look at the normal before the paranormal."

"Okay."

"Does Christina have any lovers?"

"That's a weird question from a cop."

"But a necessary one, I'm afraid."

"No...I mean, I'm not with her twenty-four seven. I suppose she could have some mysterious lover, but I doubt it. I really would doubt it."

"But it's possible?"

"Sure, anything's possible. But I think I can safely say there's no lovers. I mean, you'd have to know Christina, I guess. She's been through three really ugly relationships and the scars are deep. Romantically, I suppose you'd say she's pulled into herself like a turtle into its shell. She never dates. She never goes out. She never really sees anyone. She's been hurt to the point where she wants to fade into the background and be ignored."

Mark nodded. "So we can rule out a secret, abusive sexual relationship."

"Ah, I see what you mean. Some S&M thing with a violent, toothy lover. Highly unlikely."

"Which brings us back to ghosts again."

"I suppose. You want my take on that?"

"I do."

She folded her arms across her chest and sank back into the sofa. "Like you said, I don't believe in ghosts. But I *do* believe in Christina and I'm telling you flat out she does not fit the profile of somebody who makes up stories. The last thing in the world she wants is attention. She's not very imaginative. She sucks at lying," Nancy explained. "So if you want my take, if she says there's a ghost then there's a fucking ghost."

Mark could only raise an eyebrow to that. "Well, that's good enough for me. I don't know her, but I do know you and I trust your judgment. But it pretty much leaves me out. There's nothing I can do as a cop with spooks. That's beyond me."

"So where does this leave us?"

He shrugged. "You tell me."

14

"Hattie," Christina said, nearly breathless with horror now. "What...what did you see in the corner? What was looking at you?"

But Hattie just shook her head. In fact, she shook her entire body. She was not willing to talk about *that*, she refused to put *that* into words. She sat there for some time, trembling and wiping her eyes, chain smoking and making low moaning sounds in her throat. Her complexion was not just sallow by that point; it was the color of clay. Christina watched her, thinking that before she showed up at the door, old Hattie had made herself a nice bowl of mac-and-cheese—cold and forgotten now—and had probably planned on watching some TV. A relaxing afternoon that had now gone most assuredly to shit.

After a time, she began to speak again, going backward with her story instead of forward. "None of us liked Uncle Charles, just as I said. We saw very little of him. He was an undertaker and that...that disturbed us kids, I suppose. After he'd lived with us a year or so, it became sort of obvious that there was something wrong with him, something physically wrong. He was a tall, strange man. That's what I remember most. Then, he got sick. I heard my mom and my aunts talking about it. There was something wrong with him, something terribly wrong. And they knew what it was because they'd seen it before or heard of it. Then, one day I saw him. He didn't see me but I watched him as he went up the stairs...he looked bad. He was hunched over sort of to the side, gripping the railing for dear life. His breathing was...was ragged and I could see that his face was very pale, very sweaty. He left an awful smell in his wake that wasn't exactly body odor. More like something inside him was rotting."

"What was it?" Christina asked.

But Hattie shook her head, still unable to frame it into words. "After I saw him on the stairs that day and heard some of the awful things being gossiped about him, I was terrified. I used to lay awake in bed at night, afraid that he might come through the door…and…and put his hands on me."

"What was it, Hattie? Tell me."

She licked her dry lips. "It was—they said—a sort of a cancer, a malignant-type growth. It was draining him dry. It was sucking the life out of him."

Was that it? Christina was practically crestfallen. She had expected something much more diabolical somehow. "Did he see anyone about it?"

"No, not then. Not for a while. I heard my mother tell one of my aunts that it wasn't the sort of thing a doctor could cure. I had no idea what that meant, but it scared me. What sort of growth could it be? I imagined the worst things. Then, one day, sneaking around and nosing about as was my way, I saw it."

"You…saw it?"

Hattie nodded, her eyes bright and wet like shiny stones. They were the eyes of a teenage girl as if the very memory was regressing her. "Oh, yes! I *saw* it! They were in the kitchen. My mother was with Uncle Charles. I saw him standing there in the dim light. I had to press a hand to my mouth because he looked like a corpse, a living corpse… God, white as a ghost, his eyes bulging, his face like a skull. It looked like he was in pain and he was." She swallowed and kept swallowing, trying to keep something down. "He was hunched over to the side like I said. He pulled up his shirt and I heard my mother gasp and I think I gasped, too. On his…his left side, between the arm and hip there was a huge bulbous sort of growth. It looked yellow and shiny, kind of greasy, I guess. I saw there were purple veins spread through the thing and… and…"

"What?" Christina said, caught up in it now, her mouth dry and her palms sweating. *"What?"*

Hattie looked at her, grinning with her bad teeth, her eyes wide and fixed. "It was *breathing*. I don't know what else you'd call it. Sort of inflating and deflating like a lung. It was all yellow and scaly and I thought…just for a moment there…I thought it had a sort of human shape to it."

It was insane, absolutely insane, but Christina did not doubt it. One look at Hattie's tormented face told her that she had seen something, something so horrible that even now these many years later, it still terrified her. *More than a tumor, oh yes, much more than a tumor. A massive obscene growth that was sucking the juice out of him, draining the life from him.* She couldn't know what it was, but in her mind she pictured some malevolent conjoined twin, some bloated human-shaped toadstool breathing, pulsing.

Christina licked her lips with a dry tongue. "You said your mother and your aunts had seen it before."

"They had. There's some things that run in families and don't ask me why. They just do. The Slick men—my father excepted—have been undertakers going back generations. That's probably neither here nor there, *but*—" and she emphasized this by stabbing a finger at Christina "—that sort of growth shows up now and again and it always kills those who have it. *Always*. It sucks them dry like a parasite. But never before had it been surgically removed. Medicine had never been that advanced when it happened before."

"So what is it? A twin?"

Hattie shook her head. "It's worse than that. It's a horror. It's something that's aware, something that plots and schemes, something evil."

"A demon. Is that what you mean?"

"I don't know. But it haunts the Slick family line. You can believe that or not. I don't care much either way."

"But they removed it?"

Hattie started laughing with a strident, shrieking sort of sound and Christina was pretty sure the memory, so carefully suppressed all these years, had now pushed her quite close to a nervous breakdown.

"Yes, they cut that awful thing off him and it nearly killed him," she said, tears rolling from her eyes and a ribbon of spit hanging from her chin. "But he was an undertaker. He wanted it. He wanted to embalm and bury it. I heard my mother tell my Auntie Flo that. But he didn't embalm it. He took it with him to his room in *our* house. He kept it up there in a jar. That's what they said. Only it wasn't as dead as it should have been. It sucked the life out of him. It destroyed him. It took him over until there was no more Charles Slick, there was only a mad man that was a host to an evil, murderous thing."

It was madness, of course. Even if such a thing were removed, it could not exist independently

"What happened, Hattie?" Christina asked.

"What happened?" She wiped tears from her eyes. "Things went bad. There's no point in going into it all, even that which I can remember. Why rehash all that horrible stuff? Things happened in the neighborhood. A couple of dogs went missing. That was bad enough.

Then Buddy Prior—a real brat he was—he came home all covered in blood, said something had attacked him, something like a little monkey. Whatever it was, it bit him pretty bad and he lost a lot of blood. And it was about that time that the baby went missing. The Gannon baby, a little boy. His name was Jeremy. He was snatched from his crib. The screen was torn from the window of his nursery and there was nothing but a few drops of blood on the windowsill as evidence. Oh, it got worse and worse and people were afraid to go out at night. Some said they saw something creeping about. Then Willy Chalmers went missing and that's when people took action."

"What sort of action?"

Hattie just shook her head. "If it was bad in the neighborhood, think about how it was for us living in the same house with Uncle Charles... and that thing he was brooding up there. That awful little horror he was mothering." She shivered again. "I kept my door locked at night because sometimes, very late, I'd hear it moving down the hallway, the padding of its feet, the sound of its claws dragged over the walls. My mother said I was having nightmares but I knew better. Because it was no nightmare the night they took Auntie Flo to the hospital. I heard her crying in her sleep. Her room was across from mine and I could hear the sucking sounds. It took everything I had, but I went in there." Hattie brought her face in close so that Christina could see every wrinkle and age rut on her face. They cut deep to the bone like dark sins. "I turned on the light...and something screamed with high, piercing sound like a cicada droning...I don't know...I saw it for just an instant, something like a toad with a human face...then it hopped away...it just...*hopped away!*" Now she was cackling and crying at the same time. *"That's what made Charles put the rope around his neck! Because it lived and breathed and forced him into the most horrible things until his mind came apart!"*

15

Frank Betts sat in the caretaker's shack out back of the cemetery where the tall trees threw pools of heavy shade. He'd been chewing Tums ever since he opened his big yap and told Christina about the Slick family and Hattie. His stomach was filled with acid and there wasn't a medicine in the world that could touch it.

Sitting there surrounded by shovels and lawnmowers, bags of Weed & Feed, smelling oil and gas and black dirt, he thought: *You didn't need to tell her. You could have kept out of it. All these years you've kept the secret and kept your nose clean and now you go and ruin it and stir the whole mess up by opening your big yap. You'll be seventy-five next month. You don't need this shit. It's too late to play the hero now. It's too late to undo the wrongs.*

But no…he didn't believe that.

Down deep, he figured it was never too late.

That Christina. Such a pretty girl. Such a nice girl. She did a good thing and now she was paying the price, thrust into a horror beyond anything she could imagine. It had happened before, of course. In the past twenty years, it had happened exactly twice that Frank knew of and both times it had ended in suicide. He wouldn't let that happen again. Somehow, he would stop it this time.

All these years, he had watched over the headstone of Charles David because he knew that some things, though dead, did not rest easy cheek-to-jowl with the earth. He knew there was a foul, undead life beneath that stone and he'd always tried to steer people away from it. One act of kindness was all it took to put the cycle of madness into motion again. That day he'd been too late. He saw Christina picking the weeds and by the time he'd gotten there, well, it was too late to do anything. What was under the ground was already restless.

That thing would keep coming for her until it got what it wanted.

There had to be something he could do.

He told himself again and again he was too old to get involved, but that was bullshit. Christ, he was in his seventies and he still worked rings around the young college boys that they put on for the summer. His old man had been cutting down trees and peeling bark in his nineties. It was that way with some families. They had the right genes and it gave them longevity and health. He was not some broken down old man and he was not about to start acting like one.

Okay, he'd sent Christina over to Hattie.

Hattie would tell. She'd been waiting for years to tell the story and from what he'd seen in Christina's eyes, she wouldn't leave until she got it. Good for her.

But where did that leave him?

He wasn't sure, but somehow, some way he had to run interference for the girl. He had to watch her, keep an eye on her, save her if such a thing was possible. It probably wasn't, but he was going to give it everything he had.

16

Christina didn't get back until almost six and by then Nancy was half out of her mind with worry. As soon as she walked through the door, Nancy seized her and plied her with questions. *Where have you been? God, don't you know how worried I was? Mark's even got the cops looking for you!* But she might as well have been speaking to a stone statue because regardless of how much she ranted and raved, Christina's face was quarried from stone.

"I needed air. I needed to get out of here," she said by way of explanation. "I needed to do some thinking."

Nancy didn't like it because there was more to it than that and she damn well knew it, but Christina was in some strange mood—strange even for her—and regardless of how many questions she asked her, she received only the barest of replies. She clearly didn't want to talk and that scared Nancy because she was certain something bad had happened.

"Christina," she finally said. "Just tell me what happened."

"Stop mothering me, Nancy. Please."

"I won't. I've always wanted a child. That's why I adopted you."

The levity failed.

"Nothing happened. I just talked to someone."

"Who?"

Christina sighed, then sat down, slumping on the sofa. Her eyes were dazed. She seemed to be looking straight through the walls at something miles away. "I'm tired. I'm very tired. I really need to lay down."

But Nancy wouldn't have it.

When she got going, there was no stopping her. Christina didn't want to eat, but Nancy forced soup on her and bullied her into eating it, and slowly, after she'd finished, Christina told her tale of Betts from the cemetery and Hattie Slick.

"Some kind of growth," she finished by saying. "Something that was part of him but independent. A monster."

"That's…"

"Crazy?" Christina laughed with a brittle sort of sound. "Yes, isn't it?"

"So you're being haunted by Slick and some sort of…growth or twin they removed from him?"

Christina nodded, smiling sickly. She was pale and shaking. Nancy didn't know what to think. Something was surely going on…but *this?* It was insane. It almost made your average haunting or ghostly visit from the grave sound positively pedestrian.

"But…but if they cut it off him, then it would have went in a jar of alcohol or something. They don't cut a mass off you and hand it to you on your way out the fucking door."

"That was the stipulation. He wanted it. He intended to embalm it and give it a funeral."

"And it was alive?"

"Maybe it was not really dead. He had it up in his room."

"Oh, Christina, come on now."

"It died in the fire," Christina said. "Hattie didn't say so, but that's what I'm guessing. Charles Slick committed suicide and then the place burned down and…and…and in death they were reunited like father and son and when I pulled the weeds from his grave, when I showed them sympathy, they targeted me. You see, Slick wants not just a lover for himself but a *mother* for that thing. In fact, he wants—"

"Stop it," Nancy finally told her. "Stop it right now."

God knew she loved Christina and had all the compassion in the world for her, but this was madness. Maybe she was willing to accept the ghost-thing. It was a stretch, but something weird was going on and possibly something paranormal…but this was simply an obscenity. This was not just far out, it was the sort of thing a diseased mind might come up with. She was honestly wondering if Christina had really even talked to the people she claimed or this was all the spiraling dementia of her mind. And as much as she hated to be thinking it, she wondered if Christina shouldn't have an in-depth chat with a professional. And the result of that would probably be some sort of confinement and therapy.

I just can't accept this, Christy. I'd do anything for you, but this is just too fucked up. Weird Uncles Charles comes to stay, gets sick, has some sort of tumor growing on him only it's not a tumor but some sort of inhuman thing. They remove it but with the stipulation that he wants to take it home with him. He does. It lives. He mothers the fucking thing, loves it even, and it takes over his life and makes him do bad things and then he hangs himself...oh Jesus, this was like some kind of psychosis.

Yet, as much as Nancy could not believe it, she knew Christina couldn't make up something this freakish. Which meant either she was telling the truth or her damaged subconscious mind was very macabre in its inventiveness.

What bothered her most is that it all fit in a very deranged sort of way. The idea of that thing being like a child that needed a mother and the bites on Christina's breasts—

No, no, no, don't go there or you'll be climbing fucking walls, too. Keep it in perspective. Such a scenario cannot possibly be, so it stands to reason that Christina is losing it.

She only wished it was that easy.

"I'm tired," Christina said. "I'm so tired."

"Yes, you need a rest."

She got her into bed, avoiding the fatalistic urge to lift her shirt and see if there were any more bites, but if there were, she didn't want to know about them. Because how could that be explained by a psychosis? She had seen them as Mark Crews had. Christina could not have bitten herself that way which meant she had to use some kind of device. It wasn't impossible. Crazy people probably did things like that to reinforce their own delusions, to validate them. But would Christina really go that far? That would mean she needed to be institutionalized.

She's your best friend. Are you so willing to shut her away in a padded room?

Nancy just did not know.

She did not know about anything by that point.

Christina went out almost immediately which was a good thing. When she was sure she was really sleeping and not faking it, Nancy went out and got on her computer. She spent the next thirty minutes researching the idea of a parasitic twin to see if there was even any viability to it. There was. Such a growth was known medically as a fetiform, a fetus in fetu, a parasitic monozygotic twin. A twin embryo developed in utero but the pair never separated, resulting in the stronger, dominant twin absorbing the weaker, only the weaker one was never truly eliminated but continued to function metabolically within the body of its twin, becoming parasitic and dependent on its host for life. Another type was a fetiform teratoma which was a tumor which resembled a malformed fetus. Both were considered to be of similar origin, though there was some scientific debate about this. They both exhibited complete organ systems, torsos, limbs, even fingers and toes, sometimes eyes and teeth, even fingernails and hair. They were both incredibly rare, occurring something like once in every half a million births.

And all, she learned, died after they were removed.

There was not a single case of one surviving after it was removed from its host. They were rarely much larger than a grapefruit and usually considerably smaller. The one Christina claimed was removed from Charles Slick sounded like it was the size of a one-year old.

Insane.

Nancy looked at some photos of fetiforms on Google and nearly lost her lunch. Regardless, how would Christina even know about such a thing? She had no medical or scientific background and she wasn't some weirdo who surfed the web looking at disgusting medical abnormalities. Even though Nancy's rational mind told her that Christina was losing it, the circumstantial evidence suggested that there was something much darker at play here.

But what to do about it?

She thought of calling Mark, but what could he do or say? Nothing. Any rational person would come to the same conclusion: Christina needed help. Finally, around ten, Nancy called it a day and stretched out on the couch, fearing the dreams that would come if and when she was able to sleep.

They were going to be real doozies.

17

She did fall asleep and, surprisingly, she did not dream. About two she came awake, trembling and very afraid, a crawling sensation at the base of her spine as if an unknown hand had caressed her as she slept. She sat up, looking around, her eyes wide and bright in the semi-darkness. Something had changed. Something had moved. There was a strange sense of psychic violation in the apartment, as if there was a stranger hiding in the shadows.

Just take it down a notch before you lose your head.

Yes, that was it. That's how you handled things like this. It was probably nothing. Maybe she'd heard something outside.

Sitting there, Nancy listened.

She could hear distant traffic, the ever-present thrum of the city. Somewhere down the street, a car door slammed. But nothing else. Her breath in her lungs, the rattle of a tree limb outside.

Dappled light filtered in through the curtains, heaving shadows played over the wall. What she needed to do was to reach for the lamp on the end table. It was only two feet away. Just a quick grab at it and the night would slide away. But down deep she was afraid to move. Afraid that if she reached out, a cold hand would grab her own and it would never let go.

Come on now for god sake.

But there was no getting around the fact that she was scared. Fear had settled into her belly in a fluttering, winged mass. Though her belly felt light and queasy, everywhere else she felt absurdly heavy. Her limbs were weighty, her fingers rubbery. It seemed that she was only capable of the most delayed reactions. Christ, this was ridiculous. Utterly ridiculous, but she could not reason away what she was feeling. The terror that held her, possessed her, was huge and complete. It made her feel very small and weak.

But she had to do something.

After her divorce, she had seen more than one therapist and

twiddled her thumbs through her share of twelve-step programs. And when it came to what scared you, the advice was always the same: identify your fears, then dissect them and expose them for what they were. But that wasn't working this time around because she could not shake the feeling that someone had been watching her as she slept, that someone had touched her.

"Christy?" she said aloud, but probably not loud enough for anyone but herself to hear. No matter, what had come into the apartment, what had passed through leaving a diseased psychic trail had not been Christina. It had been something else.

Inhaling deeply, Nancy reached out for the lamp. Clicked the switch. Nothing. It could have been something as minor as a burned-out bulb, but she didn't really believe that. She had an unsettling feeling that nothing would work, that the electricity was dead, as if whatever had paid them a visit had carried a devastating negative field that had burned out every light bulb and shorted-out every outlet.

She stood up, the energy to do so nearly wasting her.

She could smell a high, gassy odor, the stink of what had come calling in the dead of night, and it reminded her of green, slimy things thrown up by the sea. She walked carefully across the room, the smell coming and going in waves. She did not want to meet anything that could smell like that and certainly not here where there were no lights to be had. She tried the switch by the door and it was dead. And that's when she noticed that the door was open.

Just part way.

Nancy was not a screamer and she was not a crier, either. She was generally tough in most things, save matters of the heart, but what she was seeing at that moment made something crack open inside her and she had all she could do not to cry out or break into sobs. Because it was impossible. She had locked that door herself and thrown the deadbolt. She had double-and triple-checked it. There was just no way it had been opened…not without a frigging battering ram.

She reached out and shut it, locked it again, threw the deadbolt. Both were in working order. Neither were broken or loose.

And as she did so, it occurred to her that maybe she had just locked herself in…in with some *thing* that was even now waiting for her. Waiting to put its rancid, doughy hands on her and press its carrion mouth to her own.

She turned from the door, breathing hard, her skin pebbled with gooseflesh. She would not give into the fear. She would not allow it. She walked back past the sofa, past the hulking shapes of furniture which looked like hunched-over forms waiting to spring.

She could go no farther.

If it's here, if it's here with you, it's too goddamn late, don't you see that? It might have taken Christy and, if not, maybe you'll be the one it'll drag back to its moldering marriage bed.

Nancy stood there, waiting for the thing to show itself, almost certain that it would. She didn't know what she was expecting, exactly. Maybe something corpse-bloated and hideous with chalk-white skin and rotting seaweed for hair, a living husk with a voice like scratching reeds.

But nothing came.

She went past the little kitchen and into the short hallway that led to the bathroom and Christina's room at the end.

Orange light.

Flickering light.

Oh, Jesus, a fire.

That's what she thought as she went racing to the end, to Christina's doorway, for she could see the flickering light around the edges of the door. But as she neared it, that gassy stink was so bad it nearly put her to her knees. She kicked the door in and right away, smelled candles. Smelled hot tallow and burning wicks.

There were candles everywhere.

Dozens of them. Tall, red candles of the sort you might find set on a table for an intimate dinner for two. They were on the dresser, on the floor. Set on the windowsill and vanity. Their stink was hot and waxy and gagging.

Christina was awake.

At least...her eyes were open.

Set atop the headboard, balanced precariously up there, was an immense funeral spray made of yellow carnations and purple orchids with a great flowery heart of pink tea roses in the center. At the very top, it said: MOTHER, IN REMEMBRANCE.

Nancy did scream then.

And maybe it wasn't the horrid, morbid discovery of that spray, but Christina herself. Her hands were folded over her bosom like those of a corpse. Her face was white as plaster, eyes huge like black moons rimmed in red. And she was grinning. A happy, demented smile of total madness.

"Christy☺"

But Christina just stared, her pale face hooked in a perpetual lunatic grin. But behind those eyes, there was no joy, there was only a limitless pain that was beyond death itself.

The phone rang.

Nancy let out a sharp cry, almost fell over at the sudden intrusion of sound. She went to the nightstand, noticing how Christina's glazed eyes followed her like those of an old painting. The hollow eyes of a puppet.

On her left hand, Nancy noticed, there was a tarnished silver wedding band.

Dear God, what kind of nightmare is this?

Nancy knocked over three or four candles, brought the phone to her ear. There was a breathing on the other end, phlegmy, moist-sounding like its owner's lungs were full of bile.

"Go away!" Nancy shouted into the receiver. *"Just leave us alone..."*

Then she threw the phone before something on the other end decided to speak. That was something she simply could not take. On the nightstand, she could see the caller I.D. window.

SACRED HOPE CEMETERY, it read.

18

"You don't look well," Christina said later.

Nancy just shook her head, saying she was just fine, maybe a little tired. *She doesn't remember any of it. Whatever she saw, whoever or whatever decorated her room with candles and that awful spray, she has no conscious memory of it.* Nancy knew Christina well enough to know when she was lying or covering up something and she was doing neither. She simply had no memory of it. That was good and maybe it was also bad.

By the time she came out of her little fugue, Nancy had gotten rid of the funeral spray and all those candles, even the wedding band. They were now out in the dumpster behind the building. Christina had watched her getting rid of that stuff with glazed eyes, but apparently it had not registered either.

"Tell me, Nancy," she said. "Tell me what happened."

Nancy just chewed her lip. There were so many things she could have said, but traumatizing her best friend further would solve nothing. "I had some really bad dreams, Christy. I thought maybe it was something else…but, you know, more I think about it, more I'm sure it was just dreams."

Christina said nothing. There was a suspicious gleam in her eyes. "It smells like flowers in here. Did you notice that?"

"It must be your potpourri from the other room."

"Sure."

Now we're fencing, Nancy thought. *I'm lying and she's lying. We probably both think we're protecting each other, but are we?* She cleared her throat, looking at anything but Christina. "I was thinking," she said. "How would you feel about moving in with me for a time?"

"Why?"

"Why not? We're both manless chicks. We can do chick things: watch chick movies and eat chick food, hang bras in the bathroom and leave feminine hygiene products in plain sight. At night, we'll groom each other like monkeys."

She was trying to be funny, but her voice had a noticeably hysterical edge to it.

Christina sighed. "Nancy..."

"All right. I don't want you being alone."

"Is that really why?"

"Why else?"

Nancy couldn't look her in the eye. Maybe she was afraid of what she might see or what Christina might see when she looked back at her.

"And that's the only reason?"

"Sure, why else? It's not because I think you're a soft, fluffy bunny with a history of lunacy."

Christina almost smiled at that. "Only you could make a crazy person sound like something you'd want to pet."

"You're not crazy."

"Sure I am."

"Christy, c'mon."

"No, Nancy, I'm staying here. I'll be just fine. I want you to go back home. There's nothing you can do here. Not now."

"I'm not leaving," Nancy said.

"I think you better."

"No."

"You're going to wish you had."

"Stop it, Christy. Just stop it."

Christina closed her eyes. "It won't be long now."

But Nancy would not leave. She went back to the couch and sat there, watching the door, thinking that it looked much like a coffin lid. But the power was back on and she did not turn out the lights. She didn't think she would ever turn them out again.

Just before dawn, Mark Crews came over. He thankfully showed while Christina was in the shower so they were able to talk. Nancy laid it out in detail about what she'd found in Christina's bedroom.

"You shouldn't have touched any of it," he told her, practically scolding her. "We might have been able to learn something."

"No, you wouldn't have learned anything. The sort of thing that came in here probably didn't leave any prints or trace evidence...unless it was a few stray maggots," she said, that edge to her voice again. She couldn't help herself. It felt like she was breaking apart inside.

"Nancy, I thought we agreed on that ghost stuff."

"No, that was your appraisal, not mine. I don't know what's going on…but after tonight, well, I'm leaning towards the non-human agency."

Mark didn't know what to say to that so he said nothing. He shrugged. He opened his mouth to speak a few times, but that was about it. Finally, he stood up and examined the lock and deadbolt. "Doesn't look like it was forced or tampered with," he said.

Nancy glared at him. "I was sleeping on the couch, Mark. I was fifteen feet away from the door. I'm pretty sure that if anyone tried to force their way in here, I would have heard them."

"So you think a ghost came in here?"

"Don't you?"

He shook his head. "I don't know what to think anymore."

Nancy gave his worn mind a bit more to chew on. She told him everything Christina had told her about Slick, the strange growth, and his suicide. Then she filled him in on her research into parasitic twins.

He was a patient guy, but this was just a little too much. "Do you have any idea how fucking loopy that sounds? This twin-thing grows out of him, is cut off, he takes it fucking home and whispers sweet nothings to it and pets it like a wet puppy, then it comes to life and…and…*shit*, Nancy, come on. It's fucking nuts and we both know it. A ghost is one thing, I guess, but this…a freak? A monster? The ghost *of* a monster?"

"Forget about all that. Maybe I shouldn't have said anything about it," Nancy said. "Even if that's crap, the candles and the funeral spray certainly are not. They're down in the dumpster right now unless they've turned to fairy dust."

"I'm going to take a look," he said, rising and heading straight for the door before she could stop him.

"Please do."

Ten minutes later, he had still not come back and Nancy didn't honestly believe he ever would. She was pretty much convinced that this was the last she'd see or hear from Mark Crews. Outwardly, being a cop and a supreme pragmatist (or pessimist), he had to look at things rationally and hold the entire twisted affair up to the mirror of his perceived reality. The only outcome to that was that Christina was indeed unbalanced and was creating the entire scenario as part of some delusional complex. That was outwardly. Inwardly, in the depths of his mind and the shadowy tracts of his subconscious where dark things skittered and nameless horrors dwelled, he knew he had stepped into something he could not explain, a nightmare world of spooks and writhing dark fantasies. He had to free himself from it for fear that if the cracks in his reality became too large he might just fall through one and never find his way out.

Which left her and Christina alone.
Except they probably weren't alone at all.

19

A week passed.

An amazingly quiet, normal, terribly average week and nothing happened. No weird phenomena and no flower deliveries in the dark watches of night. Even the dreams Christina had suffered through abated. Nancy relaxed one nerve at a time. After five days of complete tedium, sitting there like a mother bird on her egg, staring at Christina, feeding her and making sure she got to bed on time and listening outside the bathroom door when she peed and peering through the keyhole when she took a bath—she simply couldn't take it anymore. By the second day, she was relieved. By the fourth, bored silly. And by the sixth, she began to pick at Christina for diversion. Finally, it reached the point where Christina had had enough and told her to either go back to work or she was throwing her out of the apartment permanently.

"I'm sorry, Christy," Nancy apologized, "but sometimes...well, I just get bitchy. I don't know why, I just—"

"You're too hyper, Nancy. You have to quit mothering me and protecting me. If something is really happening, then you're throwing yourself under the bus. If it's not, you're driving yourself crazy for no good reason."

Finally, Nancy went back to work and it was like the entire atmosphere of the apartment let out a collective sigh. Christina was able to relax, really relax, for the first time in days. She loved Nancy because Nancy was a friend in a million—kind, patient, sympathetic, long-suffering, and loyal beyond belief—but she needed her away. She did not believe for a moment that any of this was over with. It was still going on. Maybe not directly to her, but it was there, a movement, a malefic motion, a ripple like fish feeding just beneath the surface of a dark pond.

Some things made sense now...a scary, convoluted sort...but sense all the same. She understood the undertaker thing and how this had been happening again and again through generations of the Slick family. There was even a sort of logic to her nightmare delirium of the horse-drawn hearse wagon. That was something.

But it wasn't enough.

Her chat with Hattie had created as many questions as it had answered. So, an hour after Nancy left, Christina jumped in her car and drove directly over there. As she pulled to a stop before Hattie's ranch house, a strange anxiety came over her and she sat there, gripping the wheel. *Something's changed here,* she thought. *Something has gone bad.* It was insane, but didn't it almost seem like the shadows thrown by the trees were longer in the yard? That a darkness that should have been dispelled by direct sunlight clung around the doors and windows, becoming especially thick under the porch?

But that was entirely subjective and she knew it.

Trying to control the alarm that was rising inside her, Christina stepped out of the car and went up the walk. As she passed beneath the shadows thrown by the towering elms, she shivered. Something was wrong here and nobody could convince her otherwise. Was it her imagination that those plastic sunflowers did not seem to spin even in the breeze? That the plastic ducks and bunnies seemed distorted, weirdly crooked? Or that the terracotta garden gnomes seemed to be grinning almost salaciously at her?

It was crazy.

One thing that wasn't crazy was that every shade was pulled as if Hattie feared the sunlight. Christina knocked on the door for five minutes but there was no reply. She even tried to let herself in, but it was locked. Finally, she called out, "HATTIE! IT'S ME, CHRISTINA! I NEED TO TALK WITH YOU!"

Still no reply.

She began to wonder if something had happened to Hattie so she knocked again, this time even harder until her knuckles ached. Then, she heard movement inside...a sort of thumping, bumping sound like something heavy was being dragged down the hallway. In her mind, she pictured something not *being* dragged but dragging itself, something shapeless and unpleasantly soft. Whatever it was, it was quite near the door because she heard a voice that sounded weak, dry and fragmented say, *"You've caused me enough trouble...I said things I shouldn't have said...now I'm paying the price for it...your fault...all your fault...you goddamn bitch..."*

That was it.

Christina heard Hattie moving away from the door and again with that terrible thumping, sliding sound that made her hackles stand on end. Something was very wrong in there and she planned on finding out what. She thought of bringing the police in, maybe Nancy's friend, Mark Crews, but in the end she came up with a better plan and drove out to Sacred Hope Cemetery. It didn't take her long to find Frank Betts. He was not a young man and when he saw her, he looked considerably older.

"I knew you'd be coming," he said, lighting a cigarette and staring across the rows of headstones. "You had to, sooner or later."

Christina ignored whatever veiled reference he was making and got to the point. She told him about her visit with Hattie last week, then her visit today. She went in no more detail than that. She had talked with her and now something was going on over at her house.

"You want me to go over there?" he asked.

"Yes, please. Would you?"

"Don't know what good I could do. Haven't talked to her in years. Doubt if she'd want to see me now."

"Please."

"All right."

She was amazed how easily she talked him into it and maybe that was because, as he said, he expected her. Frank Betts knew a great deal more about all this than he was willing to admit and maybe, just maybe, he felt a responsibility here. They climbed into Christina's car and drove back to Hattie's. Frank said little on the way. When they arrived, he stepped out hesitantly.

"Still...still feels the same," he said, looking around the neighborhood. "I grew up down the way." He sighed and rubbed his eyes. "I guess we better go see what this is about."

They went up to the door and Frank jiggled the knob before knocking. "Open up, Hattie," he called out. "It's Frank Betts. We can't pretend this ain't happening again. We just can't."

There was no sound from inside, but they both knew she was there. They could *feel* her inside, waiting in the dark, hoping they'd go away.

"Guess you give me no choice," he said, lifting his foot and stomping the door with everything he had, his size twelve work boot popping it open quite easily. "Cheap lock. They ain't worth a shit."

The door stood open maybe six or seven inches and beyond, it was dim and shadowy like a cellar hold. Christina could imagine twisted, diminutive things like the garden gnomes crouching in there, grinning and beady-eyed. Frank swallowed and looked at Christina, then he pushed the door open. She followed him in and immediately they were stopped by a rolling, hot stench of putrescence that seemed to have physical weight to it. It was the malevolent odor of a dozen worm-eaten coffins opening simultaneously, the smell of woodchucks or squirrels rotting to fur and bones within the walls, the stink of carcasses swollen and green, exhaling the yellow, fusty gases of putrefaction.

It was warm, moist, and sickening.

Christina could feel it lay over her skin and taste it on her tongue. She had all she could do not to run right back out the door and vomit in the sunshine. Frank steadied himself with one hand pressed against the wall. He fumbled about for a light switch, clicked it several times, but no light came on.

"Power's out," he said, swallowing as if he was trying to keep his stomach down.

Christina stood there behind him, her arms wrapped around herself, her belly rolling over again and again, bile inching up the back of her throat. That reek...it was the smell of something dead for days if not weeks. But Hattie was alive not an hour before and Christina did not believe for a minute that she had been speaking through the door to a corpse. Hattie had said she was paying the price and, dear God, what did that mean?

You can turn around right now. You can leave right now before you see something that will turn your mind black.

But she wasn't leaving.

"Hattie?" Frank called out. *"Hattie?"*

The silence gathered around them like hoarfrost on windows. But it wasn't entirely silent. Christina heard a buzzing and a large black fly settled onto the back of her arm. She swatted it away and another replaced it. Frank was waving flies from his face, too.

"Hattie?" he said.

For a moment there was nothing, then Christina heard that thumping, sliding sound again and she pictured a sack of wet laundry being dragged over the floor. She could almost smell the fear sweating out of her with a sharp, acidic odor. Frank stepped into the living room and she was right behind him. All they could hear was the steadily rising drone of flies, what had to be literally hundreds of them. The way they would gather at dumps or mass graves. The stench grew worse if that was even possible.

Christina swatted away more flies and nearly swallowed one when it flew into her mouth.

"You stay back," a voice said from the far end of the living room where the darkness was heavy and cave-like, almost suffocating. "You weren't invited in! Get out of my house! Out! *Out!*"

Christina knew Hattie had secreted herself in the corner near the doorway leading into the dining room, that she had hidden herself there like a funnel web spider webbing itself in a dark crawlspace. That was bad enough…but her voice, it was wet and mucid as if her mouth was filled with something soft and sloppy like pudding.

Frank reached out and took Christina's hand and she was grateful for the feel of his huge, callused paw, its strength and wiry age.

"You need to tell us what happened," he said to Hattie. "Maybe we can help you."

A laughter that was wizened and hysterical came out of the darkness. It was inhuman and braying like a dozen puppets giggling. "Help *me?*" came the wet, bubbling voice. "No help for me! I opened my mouth…I told a story I wasn't supposed to tell and I paid the price! You can…you can tell that little cunt with you that she'll pay it, too! Because in the end, we *all* pay it as is proper because that's what *he* wants! That's what it wants! Now get out because there ain't no help this side of the grave! The living can't help the dead and a corpse must lay where it falls…"

The voice was horrible…gelatinous and almost sort of chunky as if her tongue was coming apart in her mouth as she spoke.

Even though Christina tried to pull him back, Frank stepped forward. He moved towards the voice, then he turned and grabbed hold of the heavy drapes and yanked them open and Hattie screamed, screamed in agony as if acid had been thrown in her face. In the square of light that flooded the living room, Christina saw an undulant sack-like form squirm away from the light and creep—because that was how it moved, it *creeped*—into the brooding, protective darkness of the dining room.

And as it moved, a great buzzing net of flies lifted off it and dispersed into the air. They were everywhere, darkening the walls and congregating on the ceiling and lighting off the furniture. It was as if the house was some fetid, rotting thing they were feeding upon.

Frank made to follow after Hattie and Christina grabbed his arm. "No," she said. "No more."

But he shrugged her off and stepped towards the dining room. She saw that Hattie had left a sort of slimy trail on the floor as she scuttled away and that there were little white things squirming in it.

"Hattie," Frank said, his breathing very rapid as if he was on the verge of a heart attack or a stroke. *"Hattie."*

What happened then was something that nearly made Christina go out cold. As Frank approached the buzzing, shivering mass of Hattie Slick, she hissed at him like a cat and said, *"Away and out of my house or you'll be sorry! You'll be sorry for what you see and what I am!"* And when Frank did not heed her advice and turn tail, she crawled out from under the dining room table, a veil of engorged blowflies rising from her and filling the air like windblown ash.

"Jesus," Frank said, stepping back.

Hattie was living corpse mulch, a writhing, hissing soup of carrion steaming with noisome gases and bubbling with hungry meat flies. She was an eruption of maggots and rivers of yellow pus and puddling black corpse drainage. Her flesh was like dozens of slithering jellyfish intertwining and gushing with putrescence and giving birth to thousands of wiggling graveworms with suckering mouths. And beneath that rolling, repellent decay, she glared out at them with a bulging meat-pink eyeball that was glistening and purple-veined like an unfertilized egg, her mouth a ragged and screaming toothless chasm.

She crept. She oozed. She wriggled.

She slid forward with a sticky noise like a slug, a rotten and liquid mass of decomposition that called Christina's name.

Frank half-carried, half-dragged Christina out of there. He put her in the passenger side of her car and left her there in the sunlight. Twice he went back to the house and twice he lost his nerve and returned to the car. He was a man who was used to taking care of business, of getting things done...but now on this awful day, he just did not know what to do.

After a time, Christina came around and began to sob, falling into his arms as he sat beside her. He held her for some time, stroking her hair.

"I'm...okay," she finally said.

"No, you're not. Neither of us'll ever be okay again."

She chewed her lower lip, the pain helping her concentrate. "What about...*her?*"

Frank pulled slow and long off his cigarette, blowing the smoke out through his teeth. "A week or two...her mail'll pile up and they'll send the boys in blue over. They'll find her dead. An old woman who died alone. That's how they'll log it and that's how they should log it."

20

That night, sitting in his rocker and feeling a formless terror expanding inside him, Frank thought about Christina and the terrible damage done to her by something that shouldn't have been in the first place. He pulled off a can of Iron City and smoked a cigarette, feeling all his years coming back to him and damning him for those things he did not do, things that might have stopped all this.

It's easy to think that, he considered as he rocked slowly back and forth. *But you were no different. You wanted to live. You wanted to live as a sane man and not a haunted one and that's why you kept out of it.*

Sure enough, sure enough.

There was so much more he could have told Christina but he was afraid what the knowledge would have done to her. He could have told her about the other two women who had committed suicide when what was in Charles David Slick's grave forced its attentions upon them. But that would have accomplished nothing. It would only have reinforced what was in her mind, pushed her closer to taking her own life. Something he was sure she was seriously considering by that point.

He also could have told her about the night the Slick house burned down because he was there, he was part of it, and even all these years later, he still saw that night when he closed his eyes.

He was seventeen at the time and the year was 1956. Frank was a big, able kid back then. He had played football and baseball, wrestled a bit. He was in his senior year of high school and he had already planned on joining the Navy Seabees after graduation in May. The business with Charles David Slick had reached a sort of critical mass by the fall of that oddly prophetic year. It had turned cold early. By late September, the leaves had gone orange and then brown, blowing into streets and yards.

The leaves. Autumn's falling leaves always brought it all back to him.

Sitting there, he lit another cigarette as he rocked back and forth, remembering things he would have soon as forgotten.

Long before Charles had gotten sick and the mass was removed from his side, he had developed something of a frightening reputation in the neighborhood because he was just plain weird. He never seemed to go out during the daytime and when people encountered him at night, face white as the moon and those huge, staring dark eyes…well, he became the local Boo Radley. Very few people saw him, Frank knew, and those that did inflated and exaggerated their encounters until Charles was some sort of night-haunting spook, a walking dead man, a wraith, the boogeyman of lore, when in fact he was probably just a very odd, very lonely sort of man.

The children of the neighborhood, of course, overheard the gossip their parents whispered and blew it all out of reasonable proportion. Frank remembered his own mother shaking her head and rolling her eyes at the stories. She was of a mind that the Slicks were certainly a strange bunch, but they were harmless, completely harmless. Though she did admit in a lowered voice that there was some bad blood in their past and certain dark goings-on and that was why God was particularly hard on them, visiting a sort of punishment down upon them, but God certainly didn't need any help in tormenting them. *Leave them to their own*, she always said. *Just leave them to their own*.

It probably would have died out in time, but then rumors began to circulate that Charles had a strange malignant growth sprouting out of him and it looked a little too much like a twin to be discounted. A lot of people didn't believe that at all; others weren't so sure. The kids of the neighborhood had already decided it was a monster that was going to break free and begin a reign of terror at any time.

As it turned out, they were quite nearly right.

Charles had the growth removed. It had taken some fourteen hours of intensive surgery to remove the mass, Dee Dee Slick, Hattie's mother, had confided to some of the neighbor ladies who spread it as far and fast they could. She also admitted that he refused to part with the mass, that he brought it home in a jar. *A big jar, a big, big, big jar*, she was rumored to have said. *Had to be big because the dang thing weighed nearly twenty pounds*. All of this was more than enough to keep the gossips chattering away far into the night for the next month or so.

Then things began to happen.

Dee Dee foolishly reported that Charles would allow no one in his room, that he stayed up there whispering to the mass throughout the night. Hattie, of course, was repeating to her friends just about everything she heard her mother and aunts talk about in guarded tones. And one of the things she said was that sometimes it wasn't just Charles' voice they heard up there, but the voice of another, thin and reedy, that could not have been his.

Charles continued with his night walks, making sure to keep his door carefully locked. And as Hattie told her friends, *It's not to keep us out but to keep that thing in.* Still, nobody paid too much mind to all this. Not until cats and dogs began disappearing in the night. That was bad, but it escalated when the Gannon baby disappeared and Willy Chalmers vanished coming home from a Boy Scout meeting one night. That's when people became incensed and particularly when the police refused to tie together the boy's disappearance with Charles Slick. No evidence, they claimed.

In his rocker, the years weighing him down, Frank muttered, "Was bound to happen."

Because he was a big kid he got brought into it with the others: his old man, his Uncle Chic, Mr. Bowers and George Seeth, who managed the local A&P. They were led by Orlan Chalmers, Willy's dad, who, understandably, was not going to sit by and do nothing when he was certain he knew who the culprit was. All in all, about a dozen of the neighbor men formed themselves into a little vigilante mob that kicked their way right through the front door of the Slick house. What they did was illegal as hell, but thinking back on it, Frank could not even recall the criminal nature of it entering into the equation. They burst through the door and the amazing thing was, Dee Dee Slick and her sisters looked almost glad to see them. They were a frightened bunch and that was something Frank remembered most clearly. The look in their eyes. They were huddled together like frightened rabbits.

Dee Dee did not demand they leave her house.

Oh no, she merely pointed upstairs and told the men gathered that Charles was in the attic room at the back of the house.

Orlan Chalmers led the way up there.

The men carried flashlights and lanterns. There were no weapons that Frank could recall, save a few lock-blade knives. The attic stairwell was a crowded, narrow corridor and they had to go up it single file. When they got to the top, the door was locked.

"Open up in there goddammit," Orlan said. "Open up, Charles, or we'll take this sonofabitch right off its hinges."

There was silence inside for a moment or two and those seconds dragged out like days. Especially for Frank who was shit-scared to begin with. He was just waiting there in the stairwell, all those lights making crazy lurching shadows jump around them. He was waiting for the door to be thrown open and some hideous goblin to come leaping out at them, claws slashing and teeth tearing. But that didn't happen. The stairwell stank with a rotten, black sort of odor, the kind of moldering stench you got sometimes when you rolled over a log that had laid mildewing and mossy for many, many years.

Finally a voice said, *"Go away. You're not wanted here."*

That voice made more than one man take a step back and down. It was hissing and windy, a screeching, tinny sort of voice and for Frank it was like a fork scraped up his spine.

"Open up," Orlan demanded, but even some of his anger had dried up.

"This is not your place and you don't belong here!" the voice said. *"Get away! Get away!"*

But there was no backing down by that point.

Orlan, perhaps remembering the love he held for his dear son, let out a wild cry and threw his bulk against the door. He wasn't a big guy, but he was well-muscled from working in a lumber yard and right then he could have bowled over the defensive line of the Pittsburgh Steelers. He hit it and there was a cracking sound loud as a shotgun blast and the door flew in.

Frank saw what was in there.

In the light of the lantern George Seeth held out, they all saw it quite clearly. Charles was dead, hanging from a beam overhead. His neck was stretched like a white cord, his face purple and swollen. He swung back and forth with a slow twisting motion.

It was an awful sight, of course, but it paled in comparison to the thing that was riding him.

The thing that had been talking to them.

They saw it just for an instant: it was wrapped around one of Charles' legs.

But it was long enough to make Orlan gasp. Thinking back, Frank couldn't be sure what he saw. His mind tormented him with images of a crooked, dwarflike shape, some hideous little creature like a distorted, evil elf. Something hairless and purple-veined, a pulsating slug with shining yellow eyes and the engorged proboscis of a bloodsucking insect. A hopping human frog.

But is that what he really saw?

Even now, he couldn't be sure. There was a semi-human shape and it was small like a toddler. He knew that much. It didn't like the light. It made a sort of squealing sound and climbed the corpse of Charles Slick like a vine, crawling around to his back to hide. George Seeth set his lantern there just inside the doorway to keep it at bay, then everyone went downstairs and cleared Dee Dee, her sisters, and Hattie out of the house. Orlan told them that Charles had taken his life and that the house was on fire. It wasn't then. It wouldn't be on fire until Orlan, Mr. Bowers, and Frank's Uncle Chic went back in there moments later and doused the attic stairwell and second story corridor with gasoline and set it ablaze. The house was old and dry and it went up fairly quickly, cracking and splitting from the heat, flames finally engulfing it. Everyone in the neighborhood stood out in the street and watched it burn. By the time the fire department arrived, there was little to do but keep people away.

Frank sighed, finished his beer, and had another cigarette, remembering the sound of something screaming in there as the house went up. The night of the fire was so long ago now, he couldn't even be sure what he'd seen, how much was reality and how much was his imagination filling in the blanks.

You're old. Maybe, maybe none of it was true in the first place, he told himself but did not believe it for a moment.

Christina, Christina, Christina.

There had to be some way he could help her. He refused to believe there was nothing he could do. But what? How did you fight a ghost? He rocked back and forth, thinking on it. He blew out a blue-white column of smoke and something in his belly jumped, cold sweat suddenly beading his face, his heart pumping madly. The rolling cloud of smoke he exhaled had revealed—if only for a moment—something there in the room with him, a sort of face sketched out not three feet away from him, a bulging face like a bag of pulsating entrails and a single huge unblinking eye.

It's here. It's in the room with you.

He made a choking sound in his throat. It was very important now to be calm, to act like he didn't know it was there. That was his only chance. He felt a motion near his left arm, a rustling sort of noise, then something very close to his ear like the purring of a cat.

Oh Jesus. After all these years, it's found me.

Though he felt glued to the chair, his entire body slack and weak, he forced himself to stop rocking. He had to give the creature the impression that he did not know it was there with him.

You old fool, it knows. Of course it knows.

"Time for another beer," he said, trying to sound nonchalant but he was no actor and his voice was high-pitched and edged with terror. And the thing knew it. He felt a surge of pain at his right forearm and saw three neat little holes open up as if he had been pierced with invisible needles. Blood trickled down his arm. His breathing escalated. The pain was intense, but he dared not move because whatever had been jabbed into his forearm was still there and he was afraid it would peel him open. Claws, it had to be claws. Deeply entrenched, they were ripped down the length if his arm, laying him open.

The pain won out and he jumped out of the chair, his feet landing solidly. The can of Iron City rolled across the floor, then stopped. It was crushed flat as something stepped on it.

Frank's entire body was shaking. The air in the room had gone cold and he could see his breath. *You nosed into something that wasn't your business,* he thought and then he felt teeth sink into his ankle and with such force something in there snapped with a white jolt of pain that pitched him to the floor, his bad knee—the left one—instantly dislocating and leaving him near helpless.

"Go back!" he cried, blinking away tears of pain. *"Go back to hell! Go back where you fucking belong!"*

There was an eruption of hot, hissing corpse gas in his face as the thing let him feel its displeasure. A flurry of claws tore open his cheeks, slit his left eyelid open, and cleaved a bleeding gash in his forehead. He thumped and writhed on the floor, but he was going nowhere and he knew it. Each movement brought an agony that nearly made him black out. The thing landed on his chest, forcing the air from his lungs. Despite the pain, he twisted to the side, trying to throw it. He flopped onto his belly and tried to crawl and something wrapped around his neck. He made a valiant attempt to yank it free, his fingers digging into something spongy and loose, a cool, unseen liquid squirting over the backs of his hands. It was an arm. The thing had wrapped its arm around his neck. An arm that was rubbery and boneless but possessed of an unbelievable crushing strength. It grabbed his head with its other hand and yanked it to the side with incredible force and Frank clearly heard the vertebrae crack in his neck.

His body was cold, dead mud.

He could feel nothing as the creature forced him onto his back. *Paralyzed.* Riding the edge of unconsciousness, he made gagging, gasping sounds but that was it. His eyes rolled in his head. His breath came in short, sharp gasps. *Help me, please somebody help me.* But there was no help. There was only him lying there, broken and aged and weak as a kitten and the invisible horror that was now going to torture the life out of him.

He felt fingers that were filthy and tasted of rust and mildew force his mouth open. As one vile, stinking hand pressed down on his nose, the other yanked on his lower jaw, exerting itself, making grunting and gurgling sounds. His lower jaw was dislocated with a knife-blade of agony that seemed to spear right through the top of his head.

He gagged as something soft and blubbery slid down his throat, forcing his esophagus open, stretching it, reaching down deeper and deeper inside him, pulling a mass up and up until his mouth was filled with blood and tissue.

His body shook once or twice and then went still, his stomach hanging from his mouth in a bleeding, torn mass, making him look like a crushed toad.

Then there was silence and small, crooked bloody footprints leading from the room.

21

When Nancy got to Christina's building, panic seized her. She didn't know why, not exactly. Her nerves had been bad all day, of course, and Christina not answering her phone or text messages sure as hell had not helped matters any. Regardless, when she pulled up outside the building, something broke loose inside her and she jumped out, running through the doorway and up the stairs to the second floor.

The door was locked, of course, but Nancy had a key.

As she inserted it in the lock she felt an immense dread move through her, telling her that she was going to find Christina dead or something much worse than that, though what that might be her mind did not tell her.

She got the door open and her first sensation was an overpowering smell of baby powder. Her second was that the floor was covered in it. She had stepped right into it and little white clouds were even then dispersing. That was all strange enough, but then she saw Christina. She was sitting in the center of the living room floor, Indian-style, all the furniture pressed up against the walls. Every light was on and she sat on the powdered floor, her legs and hands white with the stuff. There was even a streak of it on her left cheek. Her eyes stared out of black circles and her lower lip trembled. She had a carving knife in her hand.

"Christina," Nancy said.

But Christina did not even acknowledge her. She just sat there, trembling minutely, her eyes shifting from side to side in her head.

She's snapped, Nancy thought then. *She's completely gone out of her mind and there's no getting her back.*

"Christina!" she shouted.

For a few seconds it did not seem like Christina had heard her, then, slowly, recognition came to her face and her eyes seemed to focus. It was as if she was thawing, melting from a block of ice.

She put her eyes on Nancy and they were glassy and wet. "Hey, Nance," she said in a low, wounded sort of voice. "I realize now that when you're being haunted you can't just sit still and do nothing. You have to fight."

Nancy swallowed several times. When she spoke, her voice had a croaking sound to it. "Christina...*baby*...oh what's going on here? What do you think you're doing?"

"The baby powder? The flour? See, it's a trap. If Charles' twin comes for me, then I'll see him coming. Ghosts aren't visible unless they want to be visible and when they do that it takes an incredible amount of energy. Did you know that? That's why haunted houses have cold spots. Ghosts drain the energy right from the air to materialize themselves or to make things move or make sounds...they steal the ambient energy in the air."

"You'll see the twin's...footprints?"

"Yes." Christina nodded. "Even though ghosts are ethereal, in order to attack you they must take on physical form and physical form has weight."

You're nuts, Nancy wanted to tell her. *You're fucking nuts.*

"I'll wait with you," she said instead.

But Christina shook her head. There were white streaks in her hair. "No. This is a personal thing. I won't endanger you. I can fight this. But I have to do it alone."

"But—"

"No, Nancy."

And something inside her was incredibly relieved. It wanted to jump up and click its heels. *Oh, thank God, thank God*, it seemed to shout in her head. *Let's get the hell out of here! Another ten minutes in this bug house and you'll be as crazy as she is!*

But whatever selfish joy exploded in her head, it was quickly stifled when there was a scraping sound from the bedroom as if something was being pulled along the wall. Terror flooded her body. It expanded like a white, electric blossom in her chest, filling her belly and legs and arms and rising, rising until it was in her mouth, creating so much sweet saliva she could not swallow it all down.

You can pretend she's crazy all you want but you know better. This is beyond crazy. This is unearthly, it's completely out of this world and out of human experience.

The truth of that was in the bedroom, waiting, plotting, scheming, its diabolical little undead brain weaving horrors she could not guess at. Yes. The bedroom. That was the focal point of this nightmare and she could feel it, she could feel the vapid evil in there leaking out through the doorway in oily puddles.

"You better leave now," Christina said.

And Nancy was going to tell her that there was no goddamned way she was going to do that, but she had turned around and was rushing through the doorway before she could stop herself. The fear inside had settled into her belly in a hot, lethal mass and she was stumbling down the corridor and then down the stairs. Her legs kept moving her, propelling her ever forward until she got to her car and leaned up against it, her head spinning, breathing in and out so fast she thought she might hyperventilate.

You just abandoned your best friend.

Down on her knees, gasping, she knew it was true but she didn't have the strength to do anything about it.

22

Inside her skull, Christina's mind stretched liked warm taffy until she no longer would have recognized it (had she been sane enough to examine it). She waited with the knife in her sea of white flour and baby powder. She waited for the fetiform to come to her. She waited to destroy it. It was a throbbing, diseased malignancy and she would cut it out of her life once and for all. Charles David Slick wanted her to mother it but she would not mother it.

She would draw it in.

Then she would slice it apart while it took physical form.

It was near the doorway to the bedroom and she could hear it breathing with a low rasping sound.

Come to Mother, little one. Come see Mother and what she has for you.

Something about that made her mind teeter in her brain and she had to suppress the need to giggle or cry because they both seemed to come at the same time.

"*Pssst, pssst, pssst,*" she whispered, trying to get the fetiform's attention. It heard her and giggled with the scratching, grinding sound of a file worked against a metal plate. She heard it creeping in her direction, maybe walking upright or crawling on its hands and knees, but certainly bearing down on her, wanting to be in her arms, wanting to batten itself to her breast and feed off of her.

Ssshhh.

It was close now.

She did not turn to face it. She did not want it to see what was in her eyes or sense the hatred in her thoughts. It would know soon enough. Closer, closer. Its breathing was louder now. It was making a wet gurgling sound like an infant. It crawled around her, circling her like an animal, careful, very careful, for when it took on physical form it was vulnerable as any other creature. Its atoms could be dispersed and it knew it.

Christine flinched as it scraped its nails over the back of her hand. Its snout sniffed her kneecap, pushing slowly, slowly between her legs, seeking the source, the dark, hot, mystical godhead that brings life into the world.

She lunged, seizing it in her hands.

"GOT YOU! GOT YOU! I GOT YOU, YOU LITTLE FUCKING MONSTER AND THERE'S NOTHING YOU CAN DO ABOUT IT!" she screamed at it and it rolled in her grip like an oily fish, but she would not let it go, not until its darting head brought a fan of needling teeth into the back of her hand. She cried out and tossed it, flung it through the air. It flew seven feet, smashed into the wall with a yelping sound then crashed to the floor where it rolled through the powder, trying to escape.

She saw it now.

It was dusted white.

It was five feet from her.

It was, in shape, very much like a swollen, round-bodied toad standing on two stubby legs, its flesh beaded and lumpy. Two long rawboned arms hung at its sides, the fingers so fine and sharp they could have picked locks. Its head hung off to the side as if its neck was broken, a bulbous ball of flesh, bifurcated at the top of the skull like a brain. It had a distended, puckering mouth. One eye was shriveled shut like a set of lips and the other was huge and wet and unblinking like a shining lens. Already, the powder was disappearing in places as the fetiform's secretions absorbed it.

Christina went after it, slashing with the knife. She felt the blade cut into the fetiform's back as if it was a bag filled with jelly. It cried out, hopped away, then turned to fight. It came at her with a flurry of claws and she took two of its fingers off with the knife. They came free with a spray of juice, writhing on the floor like living, jointed needles. It squealed and ran off, more powder clinging to it, making it look almost like some puffy little boy made of dough.

Christina went after it.

She had no fear of it now that it was revealed, now that it had a form she could fight. Inside, she raged and hated and lusted for its destruction. It scampered away into the bathroom and she went after it. She stormed through the doorway, breathing hard, the knife in her hand shaking. She didn't see it. Not at first. She saw its splay-foot tracks disturbing the powder on the floor.

Had it leaped into the tub?

Hidden behind the toilet?

No, it jumped out of the corner, hitting her with incredible force and knocking her to the side. Her feet slipped on the powder and she cracked her head against the toilet. The knife clattered from her hands and the thing was on her as her head spun at the edge of consciousness. It jumped up and down on her belly, knocking the wind from her and then its hot, flaccid mouth was at her throat, a ring of teeth piercing the flesh and an incredible suction drawing the blood from her. She took hold of it. It was like some wriggling, greasy worm and she couldn't tear it free. As it sucked her life away, she forced herself up onto her knees, then her feet, and threw herself at the wall, smashing the creature with her weight. She could feel it bulge beneath her from the impact like a water balloon.

But it released her.

It half-crawled, half-ran out the door. It made it maybe three or four feet and it pitched over, its body expanding and deflating as it breathed.

Now I got you.

She came at it with the knife and it rose up, making a chittering sort of sound like an insect, its mouth opening and closing, something like drool dripping out in ribbons and making the white powder seem to evaporate.

Kill it, a voice in her head demanded. *Destroy it. This is the thing that tormented you, that slipped into your bed at night and sucked blood from your breasts. Kill it!*

It launched itself at her and she kicked it. It rolled through the powder, getting a good dusting like a raw, plucked chicken ready for the fryer. She could see its teeth now, they were powdered, too. There was a perfect little oval ring of them. They were small, but viciously sharp and hooked. They were designed to latch onto flesh, pierce it and make the blood flow while those horrible flabby lips created an enormous suction.

She gripped the knife tighter, telling herself she must not weaken now and she must not scream. The fetiform hopped like a locust in her direction, making that chittering noise, getting closer and closer. She drew it in, sinking to her knees as if there was no fight left in her.

It launched itself through the air, gliding with outstretched arms like a flying squirrel. She brought the knife up to meet it and it impaled itself on the blade, two inches of good, dependable Sheffield steel sticking out of its back. It fought and squirmed and cried quite like a baby as it got free. It fell to the floor and she stabbed it again and again and again, fluids gushing from it.

But even that wasn't enough.

Its physical form was badly damaged and she seized it in her hands like some bleeding, overstuffed rag doll, her fingers digging into its quivering gelatinous flesh and tearing out spongy cobs of meat. A cool sap splashed over her skin like the juice of a peach. The fetiform bled and shivered, sluicing in her hands like a slab of raw liver but she kept at it, ripping it apart and then dropping it to the floor where she stabbed it and stabbed it and stabbed it, pinning it down. It coiled bonelessly, squirting out geysers of hot, rank juice until its claws stopped slashing and its mouth stopped puckering and its rubbery mutilated mass finally went still with a long, low sighing that seemed to come from the air around her.

This was the time to have a breakdown, she knew.

But she wasn't about to do that.

From what she had read, it must have given itself form with some sort of ectoplasm. It was said that ectoplasm evaporated within minutes or hours but she wasn't about to rely on that.

Using meat tongs, she dropped its remains into a plastic bag and then fed them into the sink garbage disposal, feeling a weird sort of glee as the blades whirred and chopped the fetiform into tiny fragments. When it was gone, she poured half a bottle of bleach down the disposal and followed this with a stewpot of water she boiled on the stove.

That was it.

It was done.

It was over.

It was all over.

23

No. *No.*

This wasn't acceptable. It simply wasn't. Nancy stood uneasily, pulling herself up. She couldn't turn away from Christina now. *Christy needs you now more than ever.* Yes, yes. Breathing in and out, steeling herself, Nancy got her feet underneath her and started the long walk up to Christina's flat. She would wait with her. She would fight whatever needed fighting, but there was no goddamn way she was going to abandon her now.

Not now.

She went into the building and climbed the stairs and it wasn't until she was in the corridor three doors down from Christina's apartment that she heard the buzzing of flies.

Rising and rising.

24

Christina stumbled through the kitchen, her head spinning and her knees weak. She made it to the living room. Leaning against the wall, she lowered herself to the sofa. Her world—the one she had known and grown in—had burst its seams, showing her the dark on the other side, the black pulsing anatomy beyond the curtain of night.

Just breathe.

Don't think.

Don't reason.

Just breathe and relax and come down one inch at a time, she told herself. *It's all right.*

But she wasn't coming down. Every muscle was still tense, every ligament drawn taut, her nerve endings seeming to hum like tuning forks. And she was far from all right. Her eyes rolled in her skull like wet marbles. Her face was creased with tension. Her teeth were clenched tightly. Her skin crawled in avid waves as her temples thumped with the beat of her heart. She was threaded with anxiety and apprehension, mainlining now on rising terror.

She stood up straight as a post.

She shivered and her stomach turned over.

Cool/hot sweat beaded her face which felt unbearably warm, almost burning. After she had fed the fetiform down the garbage disposal, a certain stark malignity in the atmosphere had been stepped down and drained away.

But now it was back and she could feel it.

It was as if a switch had been thrown. The aura of the apartment felt poisoned and hostile. She was not alone and she knew it. Someone was there with her. No...not in the room, but definitely on its way. Something was coming for her and she could nearly feel the displacement of atoms as it pushed its way in her direction with terrible velocity. Yes, it was coming. Something grim and nameless was striding in her direction, piercing the veil of death, and reaching out for her with cold white fingers.

It's just your nerves…can't you see that? They're overtaxed and overworked and laid raw. You're not thinking straight and you can't trust what you see or hear or feel.

But it wasn't that simple and she knew it.

Just as she knew none of this was really over.

She had won a small battle, nothing more.

Destroying the fetiform entity's physical presence was not enough to keep it in its grave. Whatever it was made of—ghost flesh, ectoplasm, some material she could not even guess at—it would regenerate itself endlessly as it had on the bodies of the Slick family, recycling itself again and again into a semi-corporeal shell for the little horror to inhabit. And it would continue to do so as long as its deathless psychic matter continued to exist. Because at its core, it was an elemental and you couldn't kill it any more than you could kill fire, rain, or wind. It was cyclical and beyond death.

These were the thoughts that raced through her mind and by the time she realized she was indeed thinking them, she was already walking to the bedroom door.

But her feet moved her ever closer, stepping through the drift of flour. Her legs were white with it right up to her calves. And try as she might, she couldn't stop her own forward progression—she was drawn closer and closer to the door and what waited on the other side.

But she wasn't opening it.

What was in there was opening it.

Hot spikes driven painfully into her chest, the door swung open and a wave of sweet, filthy putrescence blew in and encompassed her. And with it came the flies, a swarming, buzzing mass of meat flies, thousands of them, a funneling blizzard of biting, hungry flies that covered her and filled the room, getting into her mouth and up her nose, getting crushed between her teeth like ripe berries. They enveloped her as if she were ripening carrion. She was there and then she was gone, buried alive in them, a sculpture of vermin.

The form beyond the threshold that she had first seen at the cemetery had come for her and it didn't come alone. It reached out for her and drew her towards it, into the storm of flies that covered it in a black, buzzing cloud. She nearly sank into its soft, mucid flesh as it pressed her closer, something puffy and clawing sliding up under her shirt towards her breasts. As the fetiform suckled her, she heard the near-constant drone of her own screams as Slick pressed his bloated corpse face to her own, but by then his maggoty lips had suctioned over her mouth and a tongue like a swollen, undulant graveworm slid into her mouth, fillir.g it. Not that there was much room in there with the mulling flies.

25

The next afternoon, there was little Nancy could tell them that made any sense. Maybe it was the medication she was under or the nervous strain. But they kept trying despite what her doctor told them. Mark Crews was there at the hospital along with another detective named Stilsen, a hard man used to seeing very hard things. Crews did not like how Nancy looked—her eyes were bleeding sores, her greasy tangled hair streaked white, her mouth frozen in a perpetual toothy grimace. She started at the slightest sound, clutching the bed sheets to her like a child afraid of what lurked under the bed.

"Nancy?" Mark said, something in his voice cracking. "It's okay. It's me. It's Mark. I won't hurt you."

Stilsen had no such compunctions. "We need answers, miss, we need them badly. We need to know about a woman named Christina Fortenay. She was your friend. We need to know what happened to her. Do you understand?"

Nancy didn't seem to. Stilsen told her what they found at Christina's apartment, that small white box on her bed with the attached card that said, PRETTIES FOR YOU. He also told her what was inside that box.

"Fingers," he said. "Two white, decayed fingers somebody cut off a corpse."

"A gift," Nancy said, giggling now, drool running down her chin.

"A gift?" He looked from the mad woman to Crews. "You hear that? A gift, she says. You wanna tell me what kind of gift that might be?"

"A wedding present," was all Crews could say, the madness in him now, too.

And Nancy sat there, repeating it all again as she had so many times already:

"There was a sound...a scratching, a breathing, a movement...I heard the flies. I walked into the living room and there were flies. Did I tell you about the flies? Thousands of flies, a cloud of black flies, fat bluebottle flies juicy as blackberries...buzzing and buzzing and buzzing. So many flies. What did those flies want? Why did they come? Why did they fill the room and settle over my face and hands, crawling and crawling and buzzing and nipping? And why were those church bells ringing?"

"Jesus Christ," Stilsen said. "This is pointless. This broad is cracked."

Crews went over there, took one of Nancy's hands, noting that it was cool and smooth like marble. Her eyes were wide and haunted. Those eyes had seen so much, absorbed so much, that what was behind them had gone to a shapeless warm jelly.

"Nancy," he said finally, "listen to me. We need to know where Christina is, what happened to her. I'm your friend, you can tell me."

Nancy smiled. "You know. You know very well where she is. Where else would a bride go on her wedding night?"

"Tell me," Crews said. "Just tell me."

"To the graveyard," she said.

Stilsen waded back in now. "The graveyard? What's this shit about? What the hell are you talking about?"

Nancy just stared, confused. "I took them there. Yes, I took them there. I was at the wedding. I drove the hearse. I saw them climb into the box down in the hole. They made a lovely couple."

"Jesus Christ," Stilsen said.

"Then what, Nancy?" Crews asked.

"Then? Why I buried them, of course."

The questioning went on but they got nothing and Crews feared that they never would. Nancy was stark raving mad. Whatever had happened, it had stripped her gears. Completely. There was little to do but keep her sedated and comfortable as she slapped at imaginary flies and rambled on mindlessly about cerecloth bridal gowns and silken marriage beds, the gnawing of graveyard rats and the kiss of the worm.

Her mind fed upon itself, devouring ebon meat and blood and marrow, filling its hollow and dusty belly, giving birth to a shivering, mewling darkness that swamped her world. It spilled from nighted arteries in pools and rivers and bogs, sinking her sanity in a shroud of perpetual murk.

But she couldn't put any of that into words, words they would understand. So she just waited. Waited for night to fall. Because it was then that Christina would come to her in a seam of graveyard moonlight, clods of soil dropping from her filthy burial gown, rats busily gnawing at what was beneath. Her grimy hair writhing with maggots, her flyspecked face a swollen, grotesque white sack blackening at the mouth, she would grin with juicy red lips, clutching some bloated creeping little horror to her breast.

"Nancy," she would say, her mouth glistening with squirming larva. "So kind. So caring. What a fine mother you shall be."

Hysterical, cackling, clawing at the bulbous bodies of nipping flies, Nancy waited for Christina to offer her a fleshless hand and tell her that the time of entombment had come, when she would be remade in death, into soil and mold and cold sightless clay, a charnel womb that would bring forth the suckling hordes of the grave.

About the Author

Tim Curran is the author of the novels *Skin Medicine, Hive, Dead Sea, Resurrection, Hag Night, Skull Moon, The Devil Next Door, Doll Face, Afterburn, House of Skin,* and *Biohazard.* His short stories have been collected in *Bone Marrow Stew* and *Zombie Pulp.* His novellas include *The Underdwelling, The Corpse King, Puppet Graveyard, Worm,* and *Blackout.* His short stories have appeared in such magazines as *City Slab, Flesh&Blood, Book of Dark Wisdom,* and *Inhuman,* as well as anthologies such as *Shadows Over Main Street, Eulogies III,* and *October Dreams II.* His fiction has been translated into German, Japanese, Spanish, and Italian. Find him on Facebook at: https://www.facebook.com/tim.curran.77

Bibliography

Novels

Afterburn
Biohazard
Cannibal Corpse
Dead Sea
Doll Face
Graveworm
Grim Riders
Grimweave
Hag Night
Hive
Hive 2: The Spawning
House of Skin
Long Black Coffin
Monstrosity
Nightcrawlers
Resurrection
Skin Medicine
Skull Moon
Terror Cell
The Devil Next Door

Novellas

Blackout
Corpse Rider
Deadlock
Fear Me
Headhunter
Leviathan
Puppet Graveyard
Sow
Tenebris
The Corpse King
The Underdwelling
Toxic Shadows
Worm

Collections

Bone Marrow Stew
Here There be Monsters
Zombie Pulp

Curious about other Crossroad Press books?
Stop by our site:
http://store.crossroadpress.com
We offer quality writing
in digital, audio, and print formats.

www.ingramcontent.com/pod-product-compliance
Lightning Source LLC
Chambersburg PA
CBHW022042170626
46808CB00003B/1332